THE
ARMCHAIR
DETECTIVE
LIBRARY

HOLIDAY FOR HAVOC

John Jakes began his career as a mystery writer before turning to such bestselling historical novels as *North and South* and *California Gold*, upon which his popular reputation rests.

Holiday for Havoc is the third of four adventures featuring the diminutive private investigator with flaming red hair and a taste for outrageous adventure.

Published originally as a paperback by Belmont books in 1963, this edition marks the first hardcover appearance of *Holiday for Havoc*.

HOLIDAY FOR HAVOC

JOHN JAKES

THE
ARMCHAIR
DETECTIVE
LIBRARY

BEVERLY HILLS PUBLIC LIBRARY
444 NORTH REXFORD DRIVE
BEVERLY HILLS, CALIFORNIA 90210

Published simultaneously in trade, collector and limited editions
by The Armchair Detective Library in March 1991.
ISBN 0-922890-75-7 Trade $17.95
0-922890-76-5 Collector $25
0-922890-77-3 Limited $75
1 3 5 4 2

The Armchair Detective Library
129 West 56th Street
New York, New York 10019–3881

Library of Congress Cataloging–in–Publication Data
Jakes, John, 1932–
[Johnny Havoc and the doll who had "it"]
Holiday for Havoc / John Jakes
p. cm.
Originally published as: Johnny Havoc and the doll who had "it".
I. Title.
PS3560.A37H65   1991
813'.54—dc20   90–26087

HOLIDAY FOR HAVOC

INTRODUCTION

Without good editors, it's hard to have unusual books, or happy authors.

Oh, books can be published, all right. Authors can receive and cash checks. But what happens if an author bangs off a manuscript without being absolutely sure whether he's got something worth anything? And what if it's sort of unconventional—not exactly what they're publishing these days?

Without a good editor to go to bat for a manuscript like that—persuade the editorial committee, or the boss, or whoever, that here is something quirky but maybe worth doing—you as a reader will be stuck with what my late Mother used to call (heaven knows why) "the same old seventy-six". Books from the factory; books like little sausages, one after another, never varying.

I had a couple of stalwart editors who took a chance on me back in the 1960's, when I first came up with the pint-size private eye inhabiting these occasionally none-too-serious pages.

Scott Meredith, my agent in those days, showed the first Havoc novel a few times, but nobody bit. Just a little too off-trail, Scott concluded. But he and his staff believed in marketing a script until the paper almost literally fell apart. Why not? If an old publishing house wouldn't say yes, there was always a new one coming along, or new people at editorial desks who weren't around when the script was submitted last month.

Hence the first Havoc novel arrived at a small, relatively new paperback house called Belmont Books. And the miracle happened. The first editor who read it, Gail Morrison (then Gail Wendroff) recommended it to the editorial director, Sam Post, and he liked it enough to say they should take a chance on it.

A year or so later, I was in New York and had an opportunity to meet Sam and Gail and express my thanks. I remember Sam smiling in a vague way and saying he couldn't exactly say why he liked Johnny Havoc, but he did, and that was good enough for him. Through three more books, before Belmont fell on hard times and faded away, that was good enough for him, and for Gail.

Just a few weeks ago I tracked Gail down and asked her if she had any recollections about the circumstances of that first sale. She replied, very generously:

"There are a few advantages to being an editor at a small publishing house, and the most exciting is the discovery of new or young talent. To find an author whose writing is exciting, bright and fresh, to be among the first to read the words of a writer that you feel is one among thousands who truly deserves to be published—this is what makes an outstanding event in an editor's life.

"When Scott Meredith brought in the first of John Jake's slightly wacky Johnny Havoc novels, I knew Jakes fulfilled all the criteria and then some. As I watched John's career skyrocket later, I always smiled and said, 'I knew it.'"

Whew. Kind words; and not a penny paid for the endorsement, I assure you.

It reinforces my point that without a sudden synergistic bond between a writer and his or her editor, not much happens. Not much that's unconventional and new, anyway. With Sam and Gail, I was lucky. Actually I've been lucky throughout most of my career, working with a large number of talented, quite different, but uniformly fine editors.

In my science fiction days, I was encouraged and brought along by Don Wollheim and Kathy Malley (Don bought my first paperback historical novels, too).

In my *Kent Family Chronicles* days, Marla Ray, Ann Kearns and Beverly Lewis honed the manuscripts and figuratively cooled my fevered brow when the marketplace kept demanding the next Kent novel faster than I could in conscience produce it.

In my HBJ days, Willa Perlman and Rubin Pfeffer helped me conceive and write a children's book of which I've been inordinately proud every since. And on the three *North and South* novels, I had the great good fortune to be edited by one of the finest in the profession; one of its peerless gentlemen. Julian Muller. He became, in short order, my trusted adviser, my beloved friend—very nearly a second father.

On the other hand, an editor can be a disaster. I've had some experience of that, too. This is not always the best of all possible worlds.

But even the worst experience validates my contention that good editors make all the difference. Editors made the difference with Johnny Havoc at Belmont—and the same holds true here.

Otto Penzler, a friend before he became an editor and publisher of mine, really liked the oddball Havoc stories, and asked if he could reprint them. His associate editor, Ed Strosser, has seen the books through their new versions in exemplary style.

So you see, I've been lucky again. I thank all of my good editors, right down to the newest, for having faith in me through the years. It's truly the engine that has kept me going.

John Jakes
The New House
Hilton Head Island
South Carolina
December 10, 1990

HOLIDAY FOR HAVOC

I NEVER SAW the giant with the cannon sneak up on me because, like an idiot, I was trying to do a good job.

"Ho, ho, ho! Merry Christmas! Donate to the Shining Light Mission, folks? Ho, ho, ho!"

The corner to which I'd been assigned had a lot of traffic, pedestrian and otherwise. It was around six o'clock on a damp, cold evening only a few days before that grandest of all consumer spending festivals, Yule. Holiday lanterns erected by the Chamber of Commerce hung from the mercury poles. "Deck the Halls" dinned from loudspeakers. Shoppers rushed. All the stores, including Osterwald's, the mammoth department emporium on the next block, glowed with lights.

And there I was, tripod and painted red pot and placard and phony paunch under red velveteen and a long white beard very tangy with mothballs, trying to hustle a little green legitimately (well, more or less) to take care of my sadly unpaid bills and living expenses, when I'm jabbed in the backbone with something hard and lethal-feeling.

"Ho, ho, ho, donate to the—*wulp*."

The bulls again? Only moments after coming on duty at five, I'd had a visit from my nemesis, Detective First Grade FitzHugh Goodpasture, and it had unnerved me somewhat. Maybe that's why I didn't notice the goon sliding up behind me.

But I certainly noticed that rod in my vertebrae.

"You can strike the set, wart," he said behind me.

He slid around in front of me. Not one of the hustling, bustling shoppers paid the slightest heed. (They hadn't been paying much heed for the last hour, either. So far I had only thirty-five cents and a rusty Grover Cleveland

5

button in the pot.) This can't be happening, thought I. Not on a public street.

But the street was so public, nobody was worrying about one more Santa Claus. Not even the traffic cop out in the middle of the intersection. He was wholly occupied with the bumper-to-bumper rush hour jam.

The giant carried his right hand in his pocket, curled around the iron job, whose nature was all too clear. His left hand dragged out a quarter and flipped it into the pot where it went *whaaang*. He sniggered:

"You're out of business for the evening."

He had a cold, narrow face, icy blue eyes and crinkled blond hair. My neck craned staring up at him. He was a good foot taller than my own five feet and one inch.

"Listen," I mumbled, "is this a stickup? If so, why did you put money—?"

"Shut up. And wipe off that dumb look. Don't pretend you don't recognize me. I'm Alfie."

I wondered whether he was some sort of maniac let loose in an excess of Christmas generosity. "Alfie? Alfie who?"

He crowded close, jabbing the cannon at me through the cashmere coat. "Listen, smart aleck, you better—" Abruptly he went blank, licked his lips, peered over as if mentally measuring my height. "Wait a second. You don't look like—"

Glancing right and left, he spotted the black mouth of an alley a few paces away.

"Down there," he said. "Dark and restful. And I can tear off that white chin jazz and check you."

I almost wished Detective Goodpasture would come back. *Almost.*

"This is a dreadful mistake. Obviously you have the wrong Claus. I mean, with so many red suits everywhere, on every corner practically—"

He checked the intersection signs. "It's the right corner. Can the talk and start moving, Todd."

"Todd! I'm not Todd. My name is—*garf*."

The last word shot out when he stepped over as though to examine the contents of my receptacle and used the move to cover a gouge of my ribs with his hidden muzzle. All at once I realized this clown was not playing for

6

nickels. His blue eyes had the boiled, purposeful look of a killer who savors his work.

Alfie chuckled. "Thinking of yelling? Wouldn't. Hate to brag, but I was a crack shot in the Army. Very fast reflexes. Very fast. Care to test?"

Miserably I folded up my tripod and stuck my Shining Light Mission placard in the pot. "Thanks, but I'd rather see the alley."

Down in the alley, I figured, I might have a chance to glib-tongue him out of what was, to put it mildly, an unfortunate mixup. Among crowds he might grow edgy and pump me full of lead Christmas presents. So I trundled obediently along to the alley mouth and turned in.

Dark in there, all right. Our footsteps slithered in slush. As I marched I got sore as hell over the insufferable sureness of the big goon. It's a natural reflex of mine. Such tough types think a short guy is automatically a nitwit or a weakling or both.

Alfie snagged my collar again and took out his lethal tool, a large blue Army pistol.

"Listen, if you're hunting Basil Todd, that's not me."

"I figured that out already," Alfie sneered. He raked me up and down with those blue marble eyes. "You're too short. I could cream you with three fingers. Ditch the beard."

"The hell I will."

He spoke low and earnestly: "Wart, I believe I explained on the sidewalk that my reflexes are very quick. The very slightest thing and I'm liable to explode like a bomb."

"Bet you'd enjoy it, too, you sadistic sonofabitch."

Unfortunately that remark happened to be one of those slightest things he mentioned. It denotated him fully.

He lammed me across the chin with the rod. I fell. He caught my whiskers and broke the elastic, which lacerated my earlobe as I hit the pavement in a heap. The tripod fell on top of me. He lowered a sole and mashed the collection pot into my midsection. I spat out the rusty Grover Cleveland badge while some small change rained on my face.

"Start again, wart. Where's Todd?"

7

Damned if I'd tell him. "Todd? Todd? I don't know any—"

Bop.

I lost some tooth enamel when he kicked me that time. My gums smarted. I vowed that if the bastard ever lifted his mastodon's foot, I'd give him a run for his money.

Sure you know who Todd is," he purred. "Todd said he'd be on that corner tonight, wearing a Santa suit and collecting. You're not Todd. But you got the suit. And the corner. So you must have arranged the switch. Where is he?"

"Floating down the Yangtze in an opium barge. How the hell should I know?"

"Want this?" He referred to the muzzle which he pressed against my nose. "Unless you answer me, you'll be swallowing one of the fine products of Remington Arms."

All sorts of wild thoughts churned in my conk. What the hell was my friend Basil Todd the muralist mixed into? Was Alfie a professional gun? I knew most of them in the city by rep, but I'd never heard of him.

"What's your name?" He gigged me. "Goddam it, your name!"

"Johnny Havoc."

"Are you part of the dirty game too? Backing Todd's play?"

"For God's sake stop gouging my bladder."

"I'll gouge a lot worse than that if you don't tell me who has the envelope right now."

Now he really had me baffled. "Envelope? I don't know anything about—"

"Who typed out those three pages? You? Who wrote the note that went with them? Who sent Todd to deliver the package?" He fastened a hand like a vise on my jaw. "In about ten seconds I'm going to start demolishing, wart."

"So demolish! That's my corner out there, I'm the Santa Claus assigned by the Nedrow Holi—by the people who do the assigning and I don't have any damned information about anybody named Basil Todd. Maybe," I suggested slyly, "if you told me what this is all about, I could be more helpful."

8

Alfie hesitated, still grasping my chin like a cutlet. I'd be damned if I'd let such a loony killer learn Basil's whereabouts, no matter what Basil had done. Alfie's jabber about an envelope, three typed pages, a note, meant exactly nothing, but while I don't ordinarily look out for others ahead of number one, the creep had raised my ire with his remarks about my size.

Alfie meditated darkly a second longer. "Awright, let's go at it again. Where does Todd live?"

"Haven't I made it perfectly clear that I don't know one lousy, miserable thing about—"

That lit his fuse all over again.

He leaped up, pushed his foot down on my knuckles and crunched it around for maximum effect. Red rockets went off between my ear canals. With my good hand I grabbed the end of the tripod and shoved it like a spear up under his jaw.

He cursed, dropped the pistol. I hopped up. I snapped off the swivel of the collection pot, swung the pot by the chain, advancing.

"By God I may not be large enough to take you, Alfie, but I can sure as hell try."

He dove for the pistol while I swung the pot around and around and let it fly like little David's slingshot. Alfie ducked, grabbing the rod. The pot sailed over his head, clanged away down the alley. I charged.

I butted him, rocking him back a step. The Army pistol flashed in his hand. I danced away, fearful of having the cannon discharge against my person from an accidental bump. I'd forgotten all about the slush.

There followed a thrilling vision of the world rotating in a circle as my oilcloth boots slid out from under in the sloppy stuff. The distant lights of the Christmas decorations on the street spun like pinwheels. *Clonk.* I was on my fanny in the goo.

Alfie sucked in deep breaths. The alley reeked of dampness and motor oil. He lifted his foot again.

"Gotcha, you little punk!"

Down came his limb with crushing force. I went *oof* and from that point things went downhill.

Contrary to my worst expectations, however, Alfie failed to ventilate me with bullets. He hoisted me against

9

the brick wall, held me steady and began the quiz anew.
Where was Todd?
Where was the envelope?
Who typed the three pages?
Who wrote the note?
Did I?
Did Todd?
It couldn't have mattered less.

The stamp in the midriff left me with a hellishly nauseating pain and total inability to talk or move. Each of Alfie's questions was delivered simultaneously with a whack of his rod across my abused scalp. The more I mumbled, the angrier he became, and the angrier he became, the more I mumbled. One day, I promised myself giddily, the five feet, one inch champion of small souls everywhere will smite this oversized, sadistic bastard, will repay him for the unmerciful—*blooie*. He chopped me again and the champion of small souls everywhere had had it.

Jingle Bells, Jingle Bells, sang faraway loudspeakers. *Jingle all the way*YYYYYAWRK.

Lights out.

Two

MASTICATING SNOW, I awoke after an unspecified interval.

I heard Xavier Cugat playing, heavy on castanets. Then I discovered that Xavier's rhythm section was actually my molars.

Ghoulishly cold, I ached from end to end. I braced my palms in the slush, did a pushup and wagged my head to clear it. The tassel of my cap fell over one eye. I peered through a ball of fuzz at a curious red pile a few feet away.

The pile unblurred. It was my Santa coat.

Good God, no wonder my teeth sounded like a billiards

game. Of all the nutty things! Alfie had dragged off my coat. Why would he do a nutty thing like that? I wondered witlessly as I crawled through the mush in the direction of the sodden article. Identification, perhaps?

Nope. I carried none tonight. My wallet was in my Brooks uniform in my closet, because the outfit from the crazy joint that sent out Santas was not equipped with pockets.

I gathered up the coat, braced myself to haul to my feet and developed an even more severe chill.

The satin identification label in the collar of the Santa rig hung half in, half out of the lining. The label's frayed edges suggested unmistakably an angry, ripping hand.

Fancy-sewn curlicue letters on the label spelled out *Nedrow Holiday Bureau.*

Earlier that afternoon, I'd gone to the Bureau to draw the suit and tripod. I was in a room with three dozen other types while some nut with a mop of hair, Nedrow, handed out the costumes. Since I was standing in for Basil Todd, I'd so identified myself to Nedrow, and he hadn't questioned me. As far as I could get it, the Bureau was a sort of booking agency hired by the Shining Light Mission to outfit collectors and send them onto the streets. I assumed the Bureau then took a cut.

However, one other interesting fact presented itself on the label I was clutching. Below the larger name of the joint was the address.

Oh, mother. The *address.*

The address could lead straight to hapless Basil lying supine and hung over at home.

I struggled into the coat, left my beard and the smashed tripod behind, reeled back to the street. The illuminated clock in front of a department store swam into focus. Ten past seven. I'd been on station starting at five. Goodpasture had paid his friendly police-type visit —which I tried not to think about—around five-thirty and Alfie had showed up at six. He'd had a whole hour to trace a path to Basil.

The nature of the game was unclear but it smelled of violence. Impatiently I hurried toward the phone booth. Somehow I felt telephoning wasn't the wisest course,

11

but with my head aching, I couldn't exactly figure out why. So I stood and dripped slush and waited.

A newsboy wandered by, vending the latest edition over his head:

"Wuxtry, buy it here, wuxtry! *Evening Trumpet* Offers Ten Thousand Dollars Reward for Killers of Liam Sharkey! Publisher Soaper Fears New Gang War in Offing, wuxtry!"

Ten grand? That was news, all right. I could smell the sweet green ink. But I knew as much as other *Trumpet* readers about who had dumped Sharkey's remains in a vacant lot a few days before. I also knew as much about the kill as the cops. Which was nothing.

Big Liam Sharkey, I recalled, had headed a hot, powerful mob with connections stretching coast to coast. The *Trumpet* publisher apparently thought his death signaled the start of a new and gory power play, a jostling for the top mob spot. Sharkey had been killed by means of some funny stab wounds in his throat. Hardly gang style, but that didn't prevent the *Trumpet* from boosting circulation via the reward. I wished wistfully that I had an angle on the killing, for I could use ten thousand with a vengeance. Howsoever, I had other, more pressing problems.

Namely, preventing mayhem on Basil Todd's person.

I tried like hell to remember Basil's number. Something like FRamby Four.

FRamby Four what?

Pinkies poised tremblingly over the dial, I recalled it. Basil's FRamby Four number had been disconnected days ago. Struggling mural painters supporting a wife and child have a tough row to hoe.

I'd been doing some collection work. One of my collectees piled up such monstrous debts that hiding in City Hospital disguised as a hernia was cheaper than settling up with me. In the hospital cafeteria I struck up an acquaintance with one of the orderlies, an underpaid, underfed, unappreciated type named Basil Todd. He held the white coat job, he said, because it allowed him to work odd shifts and spend part of each day painting. He steered me through the ether parlor until I located my quarry cringing behind the camouflage of a truss.

For this I'd always owed Basil a favor. We met once in

12

a while over a bomb because he had interesting views on the current state of the art world. Such as, no one desired representational murals except post offices, and how many of those did they build every year? To scrape up pennies he took various odd jobs in addition to the one as hospital orderly. Santa in the snowflake season, for one.

Tonight had been Basil's first night on duty as a Santa. But he'd been unable to take up his post because of an unfortunate and even rather mysterious accident. Basil had fallen down the stairs when coming home to the loft where he lived with his wife Olive and his infant son Murphy. What was mysterious was Basil being blotto when he fell. Basil was not a man to sauce up much, and when he did drink, it was never more than two blasts.

To Basil's way of thinking, Art came ahead of AT&T. The phone company had yanked his line because his payments were overdue. And when his wife had phoned me earlier the same day, to sobbingly inquire whether I'd go to the Holiday Bureau and fill in for Basil on his corner (didn't I owe him a favor?), she'd called from a public booth exactly like the one in which I was now sitting on my butt wondering what to do.

"Say, fella! You in there! Say, is he having some kind of seizure?"

A beefy male face was pasted against the glass. Another queue of four or five phoners had already lined up. I was having a seizure, all right. A fright seizure.

The beefy gent garrumphed, stared at his watch, then trotted off to summon another of the law minions directing traffic. I'd wasted too much time already.

I rushed from the booth, through the crowd and down a convenient cross street as fast as my sawed-off legs could carry me. At a parking lot I reclaimed my heap and raced uptown with a floored accelerator.

As I barreled along, the thought suddenly struck that I was doing exactly what Detective Goodpasture had warned me not to do a couple of hours ago—get into trouble.

Because if I did, he was primed to make me regret it.

Driving like hell for Basil's, I could remember Goodpasture's little lecture practically word for word:

"What is this, Havoc? Another of your fake schemes like the Apollo Encyclopedia Company and the Solar

Heat Skillet Corporation? Oh sure, I know. You just have a habit of accidentally getting mixed up with crooked types. Do you suppose that's because you're a natural born crook yourself? I guess I can't legally run you in, seeing as you've got that license to solicit. Believe me, I'm going to check to make sure this Nedrow Holiday Bureau you mentioned really did take out that license. And I swear, Havoc, stay out of trouble or you'll wind up in the clink for a hundred years." He grinned ghoulishly. "Merry Christmas."

Nearing Basil's neighborhood, I got red-sore all over again remembering Alfie. Warning from Goodpasture or not, I damned well wouldn't run from this caper, at least until I found out how deeply and lethally Basil was involved.

There were few signs of life around Basil's apartment building. The street was poor, lonesome and wet with slush. Not yet a slum, it was trying hard. I puffed up the three flights to the loft with north skylight which Basil dignified by the name, "apartment." I pounded the panel.

"Lemme in quick. It's Johnny Havoc."

The door flew open. Olive Todd, a pretty piece of brunette equipment in a housecoat and pin curlers, collapsed on my shoulder, nearly knocking me down. She was sobbing.

"Johnny! Thank God somebody's come. I've been scared sick."

Over her shoulder I glimpsed Murphy in his crib beneath the skylight. He was waving his rattle and howling indignantly. Through an open door in the far wall I saw the corner of a mussed bed. All over the floor lay what had been murals featuring steelworkers and jet airplanes and rockets and other such. The murals had been stepped on and smashed. One sandhog had a permanent hole in his pneumatic drill.

"Olive! Honey, easy! What's this about a doctor?"

"That awful man!" she wailed. "He beat Basil! Beat him horribly!"

"A big gink? Blond hair, fishy blue eyes? Named Alfie?"

Her dark eyes brimmed with fright. "My God, yes! Do you know him? He stormed through here and—it was just horrible."

14

She vibrated like a berserk Exercycle. I led her to an ancient sideboard where Basil stashed his modest liquor supply. I poured a double hooker of revivifying Walker's Nutrient Tonic, thrust it into her hands.

"Try to calm down, Olive. How bad is Basil?"

"I *can't* calm down, I can't, I *can't!*"

She shook all over, spilling the booze. She fell into a chair. With my ears still ringing from Alfie's massage, I headed into the bedroom expecting the worst.

Three

THE STRUGGLING painter was struggling no longer. He reposed with his arms and legs flung out star fashion on top of an unfinished mural depicting a concrete dam over which floated some sexy broads with wings representing, I suppose, the Spirit of a Hydroelectric Charge.

Basil was a pretty grim sight. Purpling eyes. Yellow bruises on his cheeks. Wash trousers and hickory shirt streaked with blood. I detected a slight rise and fall to his chest. Gingerly I fingered a long, wicked gash running from hairline to blunt jaw. A gash like the gunsight of an Army pistol wielded by a slob with fast reflexes might produce.

"Basil? Basil buddy, wake up. It's Johnny Havoc. Can you hear me?"

If he did he gave no indication. I laid my ear against his chest, took his pulse, studied the shambles of the bedroom. Ripped open dressers. Ransacked closet. A chest of oil paints spilled, the tubes mashed into a Kodachrome puddle. I walked out, closed the door. Olive leaped up with a screech:

"Johnny, why did you do that? Why did you close the door? Is he—oh my God."

I shook her hard. "Stop, Olive. Dammit, get hold of yourself. He's okay. I mean I think he is, far as I can tell. I thought we could talk better if—"

"*Johnny!*"

15

"Olive, you want to puncture my eardrums?"

"I'm sorry, Johnny. But your face—"

"I ran into Alfie myself." Rapidly I explained about the downtown mayhem. I finished: "And he blabbed something about an envelope, three sheets of typing, a note. The label on this damn coat tipped him on to locate Basil. Sure as hell sorry." I made a mental note to check later to determine whether homicidal Alfie had indeed followed the collar tag to Nedrow's Bureau.

"Don't fret and feel guilty, Johnny. I asked you to take Basil's place. He's trying desperately to make money for art school. Johnny, what did that dreadful man want?"

I shrugged. "An envelope. Otherwise I'm blank."

"He was hunting it here too." She measured with her hands. "He said it was so big. What I meant was, why?"

"You tell me. From the top. Wait. You said the doctor's coming?"

"One of my neighbors downstairs phoned him. It may take a while. He has to drive clear across the city." She dabbed at her eyes with the lapel of her housecoat and thus revealed an expanse of bare mammary I felt it ungentlemanly to appreciate. But I did so anyway.

"When did Alfie arrive?"

"About thirty minutes before you got here."

"Seen him before?"

"Heavens no! Basil has wild artist friends. But not that wild."

"Yeah, isn't he? The sonofa—never mind. Go on."

"That man. Alfie—" She said it with a shudder. "—practically kicked the door off its hinges first. He waved a huge gun around and demanded to talk to Basil. I told him Basil wasn't feeling well. He said he'd feel worse unless I fetched him. So I did. Basil had sobered up some but he was still hurting from his tumble down two flights of stairs. Oh, Johnny, I don't understand what's happened to Basil. He acted so strangely when he came home. White-faced, silent. And that fall! It was more than his being drunk. You know he never gets drunk." She bit her lip. "I think he was scared to death."

"When he came home or when Alfie showed up, which?"

16

"Both. Worse the second time, though. Where's that bottle? Lord do I need it."

We helped ourselves. Olive said Alfie offered Basil five grand for the envelope if he coughed it up with no struggle. Basil declared he wanted no more to do with the scheme. Alfie then remarked that Basil ought to prefer five grand over some lead souvenirs in his guts. A familiar green and greedy monster jabbed me with a pronged fork.

"Uh, Olive honey—let me clarify. Basil used the term 'scheme'?"

"That's right. So did Alfie."

"And Alfie, uh, mentioned a figure including, uh, a five and three zeros?"

"Johnny, are you ill? That's the strangest smile. I really don't think it's very damned funny."

"Funny?" I was so excited my voice cracked. "Funny? No—uh—serious, deeply serious. With me cash is always seri—uh, skip that." No point explaining that while I'd have made an effort to discover who creamed a friend, and done it gladly and for nothing, the presence of parties with guns who tossed around five thousand clams increased my interest until it was nearly as insatiable as my creditors. Olive, however, continued to fix me with that You Greedy Rat You stare.

I slapped on my most helpful smile and soothed her with an arm across the shoulders. Since she was practically six feet I had to strain some, but it was worth it. The angry glower gradually faded.

"Did Basil mention any envelope when he came home plowed and fell back downstairs?"

"No. Of course he hardly said anything then. I don't even know what he did most of the day. Before he went to the hospital at eleven this morning he said he planned to work only a couple of hours. He was going to fudge some time off during the afternoon for what he called errands, before the Santa job. What kind of errands, he never mentioned."

"How did he seem when he talked about them? Excited? Would the errands have been Christmas shopping?"

"With what? All our credit cards were revoked ages

17

ago. This morning he acted—well—the only word for it is scared. Only then I thought I was imagining it. Oh, God, I hope he hasn't gotten mixed up in something criminal."

"Not Basil," replied I with scant confidence. "Let's go back to Alfie."

A shrug from Olive. "Very little else to tell. He demanded the envelope. Basil insisted he didn't have it. He said again that he was a fool to involve himself in the scheme, that he'd done it for the tuition money. Alfie said something like, 'I guess you're telling the truth, you look green enough.' Then he asked questions about who prepared the envelope. Basil tried to throw him out then but he was so hung over, banged up from falling—that's when Alfie hit him. Beat him. With the gun. I tried to stop it but they tipped over the crib in the scuffle and Murphy fell out and was screaming and the next thing I knew, Basil had crawled into the bedroom and Alfie was tearing the place apart. When he didn't find what he wanted, he ran."

I scuffed my oilcloth boot. "Can you trust the doctor not to ask any questions?"

"I think so."

"Good. Tell him *Basil* tore up the joint when he was drunk, *before* he fell downstairs. Above all, don't let the sawbones inform the police."

She gasped. "Why in heaven's name not?"

"Dollar bills, Olive. Dollar bills for the taking. Honey, I can always smell them. Somewhere behind the scenes is an abundance of loose green."

"There's that funny look on your face again. Johnny, whatever is behind this, it's dangerous."

"I know. But I'm greedy."

Olive quirked one eyebrow skeptically. "Not telling the police is wrong."

I felt like hell for doing it but that did not deter me. I leered. "Sure. But what if Basil's really gotten himself in Dutch?"

She thought about that. She nodded. "I'll handle the doctor."

"But you're not convinced, are you? Well, what if—" Oh, my fat flapping mouth. "—what if I split anything

18

in the way of green that turns up? Split it half and half with Basil?"

"What a wicked little man you are!" She almost meant it.

"Well?"

"The offer is awfully tempting. I don't understand what sort of money could be involved, though. Stolen money?"

I shrugged. "Who knows? Maybe Alfie has a price tag on him from the government."

"If not he certainly should."

"Right. But the possibilities are limitless. Let me nose around tonight. Okay?"

After a painful pause she murmured, "Okay." She waved. "You're welcome to look over this place for clues. Don't private detectives always want clues?"

"I'm no eye. Merely an exponent of free enterprise. But I'll look anyway."

While Olive busied herself attempting to restore order to the kitchen, I tiptoed back to the bedroom. Basil was still out. Carefully I went through his pockets. Nothing. His wallet, abysmally thin, had been flung under the bed during Alfie's search. Nothing there either.

Basil owned but one suit jacket. The contents of the coat consisted of tobacco flakes, an empty matchbook advertising life insurance for geriatric folks, a drawing pencil snapped in half and a wadded cocktail napkin from a joint called the Unicorn's Den. I was about to discard this last item when I caught a flash of smudgy pencil on the inner fold.

Spreading the napkin on the dresser under a cock-eyed lampshade, I whistled and examined a miniature mural.

The busted pencil and the style of the zany little sketches told me Basil had plied his art while drinking. With luck the Unicorn's Den might be one of the spots he visited that very afternoon. He had been blotto when he made the drawings because I recognized enough of his technique to also recognize a distortion of it wrought by liquids of high proof.

But the artwork itself was a mystery. Occupying most of the napkin's left spread was a black pirate banner

19

equipped with the customary crossed bones. In place of the skull was a chick's face. Full lips and hot eyes. The wench seemed oddly familiar. I couldn't place her but wished I could. Those penciled lamps issued a hormonal promise too strong to be misinterpreted. The meaning of the sketch was clear enough also.

The broad's poison.

Down the gutter of the inner fold were block printed the cryptic letters *AphC* followed by a dollar sign X'ed out. That notation was about as clear as Russian foreign policy.

Finally, oddest of all, was the little sketch on the right. Some kind of four-wheeled cart loaded with rather large unlabeled cartons. Standing on the boxes was the most ghastly Godawful bulb-eyed science fiction monster I'd ever seen. It had grasping claws and fangs to make King Kong look like a gummer. The creature was frozen into a posture of ferocious menace. Little evil glow lines radiated from its eyes.

I completed the search without uncovering anything more and returned to the other room. Olive had finished the cleanup. The place as it looked now would support a story that Basil had wrecked it himself.

"Find anything, Johnny?"

"Only this." I unfolded the napkin. Recognize the name of the bar?"

She shook her head. She pointed at the broad decorating the black flag. "That face is familiar in a vague way. Nothing else is, though. I can't imagine—"

"Me neither. But I'll try."

I folded the napkin and hunted for a pocket. No pockets. I was still wearing that seedy red suit, and somewhat surprised by it, too. Events of the past hour had convinced me that such a thing as Christmas was impossible. I toyed briefly with the notion of attempting to get an identification on Alfie out of FitzHugh. I dropped the notion rapidly. I didn't know any other jokes to follow it with, either.

"Olive, whatever was in that envelope scared Basil. He must have had the envelope in his possession today when he skipped out on his job at the hospital. We can check

20

that after he wakes up. Meantime, I'm clearing out before the pill pusher arrives."

Olive clutched my arm. "Johnny, I'd never go along with you in this except for the fact that Basil's worked so long and hard to amount to something, and he has talent, he really does. If he must start all over and learn how to paint silly globs before people will recognize his talent, then that's how it has to be, I guess."

"Well, so long. I'm going to check out the Holiday Bureau. Alfie must have gotten Basil's address from them, unless he knew it already which I don't think he did. Also the Unicorn's Den. Soon as I can I'll come back and talk to him. What say I call you tomorrow morning?"

"How? Telepathically?" She gestured to a pale rectangle in the paint down near the baseboard.

"Hell, I forgot. Phone me from the booth on the corner at, say, eight o'clock in the morning."

In my heap I stuck a smoke in my face and drummed the horn button while I contemplated.

Did I really wish to run along this little lethal maze any further? Alfie had fast reflexes and I had assorted aches to prove it.

On the other hand, I did owe the gunsel a score. And he had mentioned five whole grand.

I told myself I really didn't know what I was doing. Of course I seldom do until some maniac is ready to pitch me into a funeral box. But I decided I might as well be laid to rest on a blanket of crisp green presidential portraits as anywhere else.

I tooled up the heap, headed for my apartment to exchange the Yule uniform for my Brooks work clothes and start working. Not, I earnestly hoped, on my own burial.

Four

WITH MY UNDERSIZED frame encased in the Brooks rig, I hauled the heap back in the vicinity of the large downtown department stores. I cruised the area until I located the Unicorn's Den.

The leather-padded bar was sparsely populated by a few late shoppers too shaken up by bargain-hunting to make it home without a bracer. I flopped my porkpie on the mahogany, ordered a bomb, paid with a ten spot and shoved all the change back to the booze clerk.

He blinked suspiciously. "Ain't Christmas yet. Or are you spreadin' joy early?"

"Neither. Just looking for a friend."

He sighed. "Aren't we all."

"This is a particular friend." I described Basil as best and completely as I could. "Did you happen to see him in here today? Say around late afternoon?"

"Think so. Lessee—" His bulbs lit up. "Yeah, I remember him. Wild looking gink. Ran in here. I mean *ran*. Nearly knocked over a table just gettin' to the bar. Ordered five, six drinks. Tried to cut him off but he wouldn't have it. Glad to see him leave, I tell you. Hope he made it home."

Dolefully I shook my head. "Not quite. That's why I'm out hunting."

"Figures. He was completely gassed when he pulled out. Beats me where he took off to, though. I remember him because he was doodling all over one of our napkins."

I whipped the miniature mural from my pocket and thrust it at him. "One like this?"

"Yep."

"Any idea what these scrawls mean?"

"In my opinion he was nutsola, buddy."

"Wrong. He's an artist. Different. Because he was half schlocked, he was probably sketching what was running through his drunken dome at the time. If I can figure out what the pictures mean, it may tell me where he went when he left here."

The juice keeper moved a finger first to the broad on the flag. Then to the science-fiction monster. He shook his head each time. When he put his pinky on the letters *AphC,* he said uncertainly:

"That might be The Aphrodite Club. Doubt if he could get in there, though."

22

"Aphrodite Club, Aphrodite Club?" I repeated foggily. "Now wait. That's—"

"Ina Young's key joint. Other side of town."

The flash flashed. "That's it. Thanks a heap, and have the merriest ever."

I whisked out the door and ran for my wheels. It was a slim lead, true enough. What would practically penniless Basil be doing trying to gain admittance to a swanky members only club? No answer presented itself as I tooled through the slushy streets.

Ina Young, it came back now, was a sort of second string Texas Guinan during the mid-thirties. There were various tales afloat that she'd been the madam of a prosperous flesh house. Since that possibly apocryphal time, however, she'd penned her autobiography and gone semi-legit by opening her private club. I tromped the gas pedal, anxious to arrive before the joint shut up for the night.

But it already had.

The neighborhood was a peculiar one for a fleshpot, full of darkened job printing, luggage repair and back issue magazine firms.

The club itself, the tallest building in the vicinity, resembled a medieval fortress more than a place of frivolity. The windows on its four stories were blacked out with drapes. Each window was barred, no doubt to heighten the titillating atmosphere of privacy. I parked.

Trotting up under the canopy, I smacked into a white placard nailed to the thick door: *Closed for Remodeling —Open After the First of the Year.*

Ready to depart in disgust, I noticed a weak yellow gleam drifting through the fanlight. My knuckles abused the wood.

"Open up in there! Western Union special delivery night letter."

Presently a decrepit porter appeared. "You don't look like no delivery boy, mister."

"And you don't look like Ina Young, sweetheart. The message is personal. Where is she?"

"Upstairs workin' on her books. But she don't want to be disturbed by—"

"Then don't disturb her by howling your head off." I

23

jostled around him whilst pressing a bill, folded to conceal the puny denomination, into his paw. "Show me the stair and I'll take it from—*yeow!*"

I lurched back, nearly having stuck my loafer in an open bucket of Sherwin-Williams. Recoiling, I conked my skull on a low painter's scaffold. The porter seized me in time to prevent a pratfall into a tray of sludgy plaster.

"What the hell are all these booby traps?"

"Sign says we're remodelin', don' it?"

"Okay, okay. Which way do I go?"

"Straight through there, at the head of the stairs."

After negotiating the no man's land of drop cloths and reeking jugs of turpentine, I made the stairway. At the top, on the far side of the hall, an old fashioned coach lantern gleamed alongside an enameled black door.

I knocked on the black door and barged in. The dolly seated behind a scroll desk cocked an iron eye at me and said into the phone, "Western Union, eh, Calvin? Okay, he just waltzed in. Thanks." Ina Young put down the phone and glared.

"The dirty double-crosser," I said. "I paid him."

"I pay him more, midget. This club is private. Further, it's closed. Third, I'm busier than hell."

Her nails, painted a ghastly irridescent green, indicated ledgers and account books strewn all over the desk. She wasn't a bad looking number for a dame in the middle of her fifties.

"Well, shrimp?"

"I appreciate that you're busy, Miss Young. So am I."

"Crashing private clubs. Eh, Mr.—?"

"Havoc. John Havoc."

"You don't have a key here," she said positively.

I improvised hastily: "No, and I don't guess my friend did either. But he may have been here. He hasn't gone home to his wife and moppets. They're fretting."

She gestured to a chair upholstered in bloody maroon. It matched the wallpaper where imitation electric gaslights hunt. Her tough glare moderated even more and she flopped into the desk chair.

"All right, Mr. Havoc. Sit down and tell me what you want."

24

"I won't even take up your time sitting. My friend Basil Todd—"

"Todd?" One cosmetic-doctored eyebrow shot up. "Yes, he was here."

"When? Wanting what?"

"Today. Wanting work. Since we're redecorating, he wondered whether he could paint some murals for us. I told him sorry, we like the red wallpaper motif. That was that. I don't think he stayed ten minutes." Her voice, faintly whiskey-soaked, dropped another tone, to the cynical. "Bugged out on his wife and brats, did he?"

Time to sink another hook. "No, Miss Young. That was just an opener. Actually, I got pounded tonight by a bully boy who thought I was Basil. I'm hunting Basil because I'm mad as hell. A bartender said he thought Basil might have been here earlier."

"Well, junior, what I told you is the whole story. He wanted work. There isn't any."

With a nod I settled my porkpie on my skull and thanked her. Normally I would have burned with righteous ire over the use of terms such as "junior" and "midget." But Ina Young, for all her seamy reputation, had a tough, infectious cordiality that calmed my desires to get smart. I merely hauled my hocks. She was back at work, copperdyed hair bent over the books, desk pen flying, before I closed the black door.

As I drove away I decided I could cross off Basil's notation featuring the X'ed out dollar sign. If visiting The Aphrodite had been one of his errands today, it certainly wasn't the errand that frightened him half to death.

Next stop, the organized insanity of the Nedrow Holiday Bureau.

The Bureau, a vast second floor loft in another bum section, was still thriving despite the late hour. A last quartet of Santas was just checking in suits and collection pots beside an ancient cash register where the prop, Moe Nedrow, perched on a stool. A clue to the eccentricity of the Bureau's owner was offered by hand-lettered cardboard signs tacked to the dusty walls. Mottoes like BRING BACK BALD-HEADED MIDGETS and LET'S HEAR IT FOR MOOSE CHARLAP and WHERE ARE THE APOTHECARIES OF YESTERYEAR? That last struck me as sort of profound.

I was intent upon puzzling it out when Nedrow snapped his fingers and motioned.

"Next body, next body! Come on, fellow, keep the queue moving."

"What queue? Don't you remember me, Nedrow?"

"How come I should remember you? How come, with all the fly-by-night actors, messed-up Methodeers and floppola matinee idols I got in my so-called file? Which," he added sourly as the quartet of Santas shuffled out, "is one helluva mess."

His pudgy hand indicated a glass-walled cell to his rear. Several green tin boxes lay on the floor, their contents dumped here and there in three by five confusion. Then I noticed that Nedrow was sporting a hideous yellow bruise under his left ear. A wad of adhesive bulged on the backside of his head.

"What happened with the file cards?"

"Fifteen years of work ruined!" he cried. "Hunnerds, thousands of penniless actors and other vagrant types cataloged and cross-indexed according to which holidays I can peddle their bodies for, mixed up in ten minutes! What do you care what happened?" He covered his eyes and shoved a frowsy form at me. "Sign up. Name and phone. Don't call us, we'll call—"

"Nedrow, I was *here* tonight. Under the name Todd.

"Todd?" One eyeball peeked between his fingers. Then he went red. "*You're* the one! The guy the creep with the gun was hunting!"

I cocked my right fist. "Back off, butter belly. He worked me over too."

The prop stopped. "Who?"

"The same joker who visited you." Briefly I described Alfie.

"That's the one. Oh that's the bastard. Listen, Todd—"

"I'm not Todd. Sit down and let me explain."

He gestured to the strewn cards. "Explain what? It's all there. A life's work gone blooie. I'll never get 'em arranged again."

"Wouldn't you rather nail the guy who messed 'em up?"

"Would I! Moe Nedrow is an elephant. Moe Nedrow never forgets."

"Does Moe Nedrow ever shut up?"

26

"Infrequently." But he sat down. "You got lotsa crust for a shrimp. Go ahead."

He fingered his bandage soulfully while I explained some of the circumstances. How I'd drawn out the Santa suit because Todd couldn't show. How Alfie was hunting Todd, not me. How I was positive Alfie had followed the trail of the suit label to Nedrow's. That last remark unfortunately focused the portly prop's blue eyes on my Brooks attire.

"That reminds me. Where's my Claus costume?"

"In my laundry hamper, unfit for wear. Alfie ruined it."

He scribbled furiously on a pad. "I'll send you a bill. Those suits don't get manufactured free by North Pole elves, y'know."

"Why are you so damned belligerent, Nedrow? I dislike Alfie as much as you. I want to find him."

"Expect me to know where he is? Think I'm some kind of mentalist?"

"Simmer down. Just tell me what happened here."

"Tragically simple. He—Alfie, you say?—storms in here before my Santas get back. Points his blunderbuss at my navel and makes me watch while he rips through my files. When he finds Todd's address, he whales me over the dome. I wake up, he's gonesville. How come," he finished darkly, "you're impersonating Todd?"

"For a good reason."

"Convince me. Start by telling me your name."

"It's Havoc. I'm posing as Todd because I'm Todd's friend. He had—uh—a slight accident tonight. His wife phoned me. Told me you said any guy hired to play Santa who didn't show up for his first assignment would get no return engagement."

"Right, right. I got three dozen Stanislavskis in my file for every job. Or I did have until Alfie mangled my containers." He fixed me with a blue eye gone greedy. "What's your percent?"

"Sweet friendship," I said innocently. "The desire to revenge myself on Alfie."

"Noble motives. But you can't make a nickle on 'em. Go 'way and don't bother me. I got to straighten out the files. Right after Christmas comes New Year's and I got thirty-eight calls awready for Father Time."

"I'll be on my way when you tell me whether this means anything to you." Out whisked the cocktail napkin. Nedrow peered at it this way, that way. He pointed to the outer space creature.

"That leaves me cold, Claudio. Howsoever——" His finger inched over to the doll in the poison flag. "I'd be ashamed not to recognize her."

"I thought there was something familiar about her. But I can't place her."

"Not a good likeness, true."

"That's because the man who drew it was blotto. Well?"

"Hollywood," he said.

"Nothing. Try again."

"Brick dollhouse."

"Zingo! Wednesday Wilde!"

Nedrow nodded. "The same. What a chick. What a built. Dunno who first used that brick dollhouse description but it sure fits. I nearly went outa my mind the first time I saw her bust in Cinemascope. A sixteen-year-old having eyes like that oughta be unlawful."

A plaintive cry from my endocrine glands sent me into dreamy speculation. "She's older now, isn't she? Twenty-two or three? And short. So nice and short."

"Five feet 'xactly. But she wouldn't go for an obvious hustler like you."

"Wait just a damn minute——"

"Shaddup, Claudio. I can spot 'em at ten feet. Even if you were J. Paul Getty she wouldn't tumble. She's all mixed up with emotional problems."

"Oh. That's better. Fill me in. My subscription to *Stimulating Screen's* lapsed."

Warming to the subject like the showbiz insider he probably imagined himself to be, he told me: "Word is, Wednesday's gathering her strength for what promises to be a lulu of a divorce trial. Her husband-about-to-be-dumped is that playwright fellow. The darling of the magnolia crowd."

"Gulf Bayles? The one who wrote *Soiled Jasmine? Love Is a Bellhop? Wisteria in an Old Galosh?*"

"Yeah. Those were a few years ago, though. He hasn't had a hit in three, four seasons. Also he's a lush. According to what I hear, this Wednesday babe checked into some hospital here in town for a rest cure, just because life with Gulf shook her up and she wants to be in top shape for the trial. Which hospital, I couldn't say, but—whassamatter, Havoc? You havin' some kind of seizure?"

"Hospital," I repeated. "*Hospital!* I bet I know were she is."

"You do?" Nedrow was stupefied, for once.

"I do. City Hospital. Thanks a heap. See you."

"Wait, wait! What's happening? My suit—"

"Send the bill," I cried back, hammering down the stairs.

In a transport of triumph I dumped myself into the vehicle and buzzed for home. All I wanted out of crazy-man Nedrow I had—a lead. Basil working at City and Wednesday Wilde resting there explained the drawing. I didn't precisely know what Miss Wilde had to do with the mess I found myself in. Obviously she was bad medicine for Basil. But it would be a distinct hormonal pleasure to check her out tomorrow.

Prone on my Sealy, I dreamed all night of rowing on an ocean of dollar bills, with both Miss Wilde and her wide-screen bust there to keep me company.

Five

BELLS ROUSED ME. I turned over, regarded the dial of my wristwatch on the night table and practically fainted. With palsied fingers I groped for the receiver.

" 'Lo?"

"Johnny?"

"Whoever you are, nobody in his or her right mind calls anybody else at the ungodly hour of eight in the morn—"

"Johnny!" came a feminine wail. "Eight is when you told me to call."

"Olive! My God, I did, didn't I?" Yawning and murmfing, I sat up. "How's Basil?"

"That's what I wanted to tell you, Johnny. I can hardly bear to say it. The doctor thinks he may not wake up for several days. The correct term is—"

She began to reel off a collection of medical mumbo-jumbo. Hastily I said, "Olive honey, I flunked high school Latin four times. Just feed it straight. You're trying to tell me any conversation with Basil is indefinitely postponed?"

"Yes, Johhny."

"Is he really bad off?"

"Oh, the doctor thinks he'll come out of it. But it'll take a little time. I feel so miserable and afraid, Johnny. We don't have enough money to last more than a week or so."

The early hour had made me light-headed. I cried rashly, "Don't take on so, hon. Didn't I promise to split any loot I uncover? That'll go a long way toward paying the doctor's fees. Did you flimflam the doctor the way I asked?"

"Yes. But I hated to lie about Basil's accident."

"You weren't lying, Olive. Just—uh—rearranging the order of events. Now, one more question." I crossed my fingers. "On which floor at City Hospital has Basil been working lately?"

"The penthouse," she answered promptly.

"The penthouse," I breathed. "Where all the rich patients stay. And the celebrities."

"That's right, Johnny. What difference does it make?"

"It may make plenty monetarily. Now Olive, you trot home and take care of Murphy and your banged-up husband. I'll drop in as soon as I learn anything."

She murmured obediently that she would do so. I slapped the receiver back and relaxed on the pad with a mellow, bleary yawn. So satisfied was I with the way my conniving mind was finally fitting some puzzle pieces together, I decided to reward myself with ten minutes' extra sleep.

It accidentally turned out to be more like seven hours.

When I awoke, the winter sun was already slanting low under the blind. I was pretty damned far behind in my schedule, but the snooze had done me good. I felt better. I dressed, ate and bugged out, whistling with youthful confidence.

The mammoth Christmas tree atop City Hospital's

30

penthouse was already shining when I arrived. I waltzed across the antiseptically fluorescent lobby to a bank of elevators. A portly cop with a gleaming shield and a large wart on the end of his nose gave me the fisheye as I sidled toward the Otis on the end.

As I pushed the button the minion grabbed my wrist. "Leggo! I'm a visitor."

"State your business, mister."

I snatched back my paw. "I said I'm a visitor. Going to see Wednesday Wilde."

"Well, now," he said, hooking thumbs in his official belt, just like a comic cop in an M-G-M flick. "Wednesday Wilde, is it, sonny?"

"Yes. Isn't she up there anymore?"

"You bet she's up there. But she's not waiting to see you. No visitors allowed. No strange visitors, that is. The commissioner's order was very explicit. We don't want any more riots started by juvenile autograph seekers. We had enough of that the time those twenty girls got up to the twelfth floor where Tab Rocker was havin' his appendix out. Move along, now, or I'll have to get rough and escort you to the door personally."

I gauged the cop's size and meanness quotient, decided I didn't want to brawl publicly, and headed out in a huff. Outside, I gnawed my lip and smoked. With a celebrity on the premises, I should have figured there'd be some kind of restriction on access to the penthouse. But I refused to be balked so easily.

I toured the outside of the building. Too many nurses and docs were on duty in lighted rooms adjoining the emergency entrance to make that worth a try. I forged on in the cold dusk until I came to a service courtyard. A young guy was rattling big metal waste drums outside double doors.

I dodged into shadows and watched while the youth loaded four drums on a wheeled cart and rolled the cart inside. Three other drums stood on a second cart. One was painted *3rd*, another *17th* and the last was painted *Pent*. Aha!

I scurried across the asphalt, hopped up on the cart and loaded myself into the appropriate can.

The scent of rubbing alcohol was so powerful in there

I nearly got loaded on one breath. I heard the youth return. He pushed the cart inside a hall and across to a service elevator, complaining mightily that he was out of condition, that he had gorged on too many chicken croquettes in the cafeteria, and muttered to himself that "them cans" sure as hell felt every bit as heavy as when he brought 'em down.

Hunkered amidst the fumes, I fretted and chafed while we made stops at six other floors. The vice president in charge of refuse cans unloaded one at each floor, apparently leaving it in the hall for the local orderly to handle. I was getting stiff from my cramped posture by the time I was rolled and bounced off the cart. I found it impossible to remain silent. As the can bonged down on the floor I whispered, "Not so hard, not so hard!"

A strangled gasp from the youth. "That's the last time I eat them Goddam croquettes." The elevator shut noisily.

Slowly I raised my eyeballs over the can's rim.

The section of dim corridor in which I'd been deposited seemed deserted. I heard voices on my right. I hoisted myself upward just as a beefy Flo Nightingale emerged from a nearby room.

Nursie took one glom at me half out of the can, opened her mouth and fainted.

The patient in the suite put up a big squawk. Luckily, though, the falling angel's heel caught the doorstop and the panel whacked shut. A blessed moment later, all was quiet.

In another second I disengaged myself from the refuse receptacle and was swinging briskly down the corridor to the main desk.

"Miss Wilde's room number?" I said to the white-capped cookie on duty.

She scanned a roster, then my puss. "I don't believe I know you. We have to make certain any visitors up here are on the approved list."

I scowled and groped mentally. "Don't you have any approved visitors from —uh—Colossal Studios?"

"Colossal? Miss Wilde's studio?" She consulted. "Only Mr. Phensterwalde, the producer."

"Well, who do you think I am, Claude Jarman, Jr.?"

She stifled her opinion and hissed, "Suite 14-C, Mr. Phensterwalde."

"Who was that, Miss Bottworthy?" another nurse asked as I whisked off.

"One of those egotistical Hollywood types. If you ask me, he looks like a leftover from Our Gang comedies."

Flushing hotly, I pressed on to the entrance to Suite 14-C. The door was ajar. I was dismayed to hear a male voice speaking as I entered.

The sitting room was furnished as though in anticipation of the just plain folks from Monaco. Stepping to the open connecting door, I saw an equally lavish bed chamber whose only concessions to hospital routine were an absence of rugs and a brace of bronze bedpans. I couldn't see the face of the Hollywood number because a broad male back intervened.

From the rear this gent had shoulders three times as wide as mine. They bulged below his short-sleeved orderly's coat. He was contorted into a sort of pretzel posture, his arms being the pretzels. His biceps wiggled and quiggled annoyingly.

"Really, darling, I'm not interested in your exhibitions of manly prowess," said a husky female voice.

"Come on, cookie. Loosen up! I was elected Mr. Snodgrass Athletic Club two years running because of my built."

"Do tell, darling. Does this hospital pay you to perform or to clear away my dinner?"

The gent continued to flex. "You dint eat anything."

"Not with you hovering around and leering. Take these dishes away or I'll throw a tantrum like I did on the set of *Teen-age Trusty*. I'll also have you fired in the process."

The youth insinuated himself nearer the bed. "Lissen, I know there's not a dolly in the world who isn't nuts for muscles, movie star or not."

Rashly I spoke from the doorway: "Did you hear what Miss Wilde said, mister? Haul it."

Muscle Beach swung around, a platter of untouched lamb chops in one hand. He was an ugly customer. Despite the all-American build he had the lizard look of a graduate j.d.

"Go on, get out of here, Hercules."

"You're kinda a small bas—jerk to be wising off in front of a hospital employee."

"That's right," I said aggressively. "Are you the Chief of Staff or something?"

"Name's Duncan Celebreese," he growled, saying it Cele-*breezy*. "And I can take you anytime, small man. Nobody pushes me when—ah, hell. You'd prolly get me canned if I take a swing at you. Not worth it."

Glaring, he began to pile his plates and dishware onto a cart with hot-tempered abandon. I had time to notice Miss Wednesday.

She was wearing a pair of rhinestone-studded butterfly shades pushed up on her forehead, plus a nightie which really wasn't much of one at all. She said to me, "He practically forced me to watch that disgusting demonstration of strength."

"Think you're too damn swell for the common people, don' you?" Dunc muttered, ramming the cart toward the door. "One, side, one side or—oops!"

He seemed to trip, banging me against the wall. I came up with a fist ready. The smirk on his face widened.

"Oh, sorry there, little man. Dint see you in the way." And before I could budge, he clanged out, cart, temper and all.

I turned toward the bed, prepared to receive Wednesday's adulation. She was a voluptuously constructed item, all right. And all the more desirable because of her small size. Plumped against the pillows with her yellow hair fanned out around her pretty head, she looked most delicious, down to and including the two sensational mammaries that thrust impudently through the nightgear just above the blankets. I was about to make some fatuous remark when I noticed her expression.

A moment ago, as I separated her from Celebreese, she'd been cordiality itself. Now she was frosted but good.

"May I ask who in hell you are, darling?"

"I told the nurse I was Mr. Phensterwalde, your producer. The name's really John Havoc."

She smiled. "That's so nice. Now get the hell out."

"Why? Something wrong with my name?"

"Frankly, darling, I don't give a damn if it's Skywrite P. Inscrutable. I'm here for a rest." To emphasize, she gave a flounce to the sheet that made her assets bobble maddeningly. "Furthermore, I won't stand for any shyster agents sneaking in here. Even if," she added with an offhand smile, "they are kinda cute and small."

I perched on the bed edge. "About time you noticed that."

"Don't get fresh because of my reputation," she said angrily. "I only go out with all those wild older men because they're tall and handsome and I'm trying to hide my disappointment at never meeting any men who are short and handsome." She tickled my chin. "Like you, darling."

"That's a dirty lie if I ever heard one," I countered.

"Don't you think you're short and handsome, Mr. Hassock?"

"Havoc. Of course I do. I just don't think you're sincere. You turn on the charm like tap water. Frankly, Miss Wilde, I expected a burning affair to start the minute I walked in. All I get is the chill, followed by a vapid smile and insincerity."

She flung her arms around me. Her unlipsticked mouth was poised a few tempting inches away while her equipment collided delightfully with my chest. In her phoniest sincere acting style she cooed, "That's just because I have to act interested whether I am or not."

"Oh? How come?"

She shrugged and said blithely, "I'm a sex goddess."

"You make it sound dull."

"It's terrible to be a sex goddess day and night!"

"I wouldn't know."

"It strains the nerves something awful."

Testily I attempted to disengage. "Never let it be said I was responsible for any dame's neuroses."

She practically jerked my head off my neck, her wrists locked behind my collar. "But I like *you*."

"Pfui. I'm just a sparring partner to keep the sex goddess in training."

"That's bad?" she inquired wickedly.

"I guess not, but it's hell on the ego. I have a big one."

35

Wednesday pouted. "Honestly, darling, I really do like you."

"Yeah? A minute ago you demanded to know who the hell I was. You didn't like me then."

"That was *before* I knew who you were, silly." She bent over even more. "Little kiss to cement the friendship?"

My hormones were doing nip-ups in spite of my good intentions. Nevertheless, I disengaged myself at last and marched to the safety zone at the foot of the bed.

"Another time."

"You're mad," she whimpered.

"Good God, Miss Wilde, don't turn on the glycerine tears. I'm not mad, just busy. I came here because I—uh—investigate crimes."

"*Crimes!* Oh hell. You're a flatfoot?"

"Think what you like," I said casually. "I have a few questions to ask."

"If my worthless husband sent you, I do all my talking through the attorneys."

"Has nothing to do with your husband. It's about a man who works on this floor. If you cooperate—"

"—then you'll cooperate with me? The more I look at you, the more I see you're just my size. I wish you weren't a policeman." Her gray orbs smoldered. "Couldn't we—?"

"Love to. But not until I ask my questions."

"All right. What are your questions about?"

"About a man named Basil Todd. That name probably doesn't mean anything to you. Maybe his description will." I proceeded to give it to her. She acquired a phony look of concentration, possibly to impress me that she was a sex goddess with brains. I finished, "Have you seen a man answering to that description on this floor lately?"

"Let me think a minute."

My optics roved restlessly up the bed to her bosom. It heaved deliciously in rhythm with the pulsations of her gray matter. I was growing hypnotized by the sight when she opened her mouth to speak. Before she could, another voice cried:

"Mah God! You've already got anothuh luvuh!"

I spun around. The new arrival was no outraged suitor.

36

Rather, his little cry was delivered in a heart-rending snuffle. The gent was about forty, lean as a temperance lecturer's chances in a saloon.

"*You!*" Wednesday cried. "Don't pull that weepy routine on me!"

The gent looked me over, his eyes bloodshot from an overdose of sauce. "Who's this, Wednesday? Some cheap gigolo fella?"

"I've got a better question for you, darling. Who the hell let you in? In fact, why do they *keep* letting you in?"

"Because Ah'm in desperate circumstances, Wednesday."

"Boloney. I told you once, darling. No loans. Go write a play."

"But Ah'm yo' husband! And Ah'm all out of ideas fo' a play."

So this was the unblooming flower of Southern theatricality, Gulf Bayles.

"Wednesday, I implore you! He'p me out. I think it's the least you can do to loan me five dollars. 'Specially when you're passin' out your favors free."

Eternally feminine, Wednesday was once more on my side. "Listen to me, Gulf. This little—this man's here on business. His name is John Havoc. He was asking me about a friend of his. I'm just being polite. What's your friend's name, Johnny?"

"Basil Todd."

"That's right, Basil Todd," Wednesday blathered on. Gulf threw me a sharp, flighty look whose import I didn't grasp. Suddenly Wednesday cut in on herself to exclaim, "Gulf, I just remembered something. I saw you talking to that man a couple of days ago. I'm positive. You were talking to him. So was—*look out, Johnny!*"

In the process of goggling in surprise at her statement, I wasn't prepared for Gulf's sneak punch. It whipped up from the floor under my chin. Bongo, I was on my butt on the linoleum.

I flailed and cussed. Wednesday covered her mouth with her hands, then got control and yelled at Gulf:

"What right have you got to do that, you failure, you?"

"The right of an injured husband!" Gulf panted, racing for the phone.

"I'll show you who's injured, you bastard," I said, staggering up.

"You are not my husband!" Wednesday said. "We're practically already divorced."

"This yere's Mr. Bayles talkin'," Gulf shouted into the mouthpiece. "Get those policemen in the lobby up to Wednesday Wilde's suite right away, hear?"

"Johnny," Wednesday said, "tell the policemen not to come. You're in plainclothes. You can order them—"

"Nuh-uh," I said sadly. "I'm no cop."

"You said—"

"No, doll, you did. Skip it." I rubbed my eyes and sidled toward Gulf. "It's him I want right now."

"Thass right," Gulf was saying. "Miss Wilde's suite up in—hol' on."

As I sailed in with a ready fist, he fooled me by putting up no defense. He cringed out of the way, then lashed around with the Bell machine and whanged me over the head with the mouthpiece. I slammed into the wall. Gulf delivered a very ungentlemanly knee to the jewels as I turned. The blow sent me capering across the room in very unfunny postures of agony. I blundered into a corner and tipped over a floorlamp on top of myself.

Lying there underneath it, I heard birds twittering dimly. Gulf continued somewhere: "—damnyankee's tryin' to assault my wife."

Some little time slipped by. Hands dragged me up into the light. I was sure they belonged to playwright Bayles. Then my eyes focused.

The grim puss of the wart-nosed copper hovered near. There was another policeman alongside.

"This the one, Mr. Bayles?"

"Thass right."

"Dunno how he got in. We'll sure hustle him out."

"You're violating my constitutional rights," I cried as they dragged me doorward.

"We'll see about that, laddie. I told you to stay away, remember?"

"Miss Wilde!" I bawled over my shoulder. "Finish

your sentence about your husband and who else talking to Basil and—"

Slam. The door hid the visage of smirking Gulf.

On the way down in the elevator, the minions quizzed me.

"Name?"

I told them. They exchanged satisfied glances. Warty punched me lightly in the chest.

"I heard o' you, Havoc. Mixed up in all sorts o' shifty schemes. We'll have none of that here. Now, I want to take down a little information. Address, driver's license. Let's have your wallet."

"I hope seeing my wallet will make you birds realize I'm one hundred percent legit and thoroughly honest and oh boy oh boy oh *boy.*"

"Hand get stuck in your pocket?" said the other law-dog.

"My wallet! Somebody heisted it!"

"Oh Lord," Warty sighed. "He's as slippery a divvil as he's been painted, that's for certain."

While they slapped my suit, I wondered frantically about who had lifted the leather. There was only one good and maddening answer—that wretch Celebreese, when he bumped me.

Then he was a pretty slick finger artist. In fact, among the best I'd ever been unfortunate enough to meet. I hadn't felt the slightest touch. But I had other problems.

"Listen, fellas. Just take me back upstairs so I can ask Miss Wilde one question. Let her finish one sentence. Then I'll cooperate."

"You're askin' for favors?" Warty exclaimed. "With your name and record? And actin' suspicious? And with no identification? And sneakin' in after I told you to stay out? Nary a chance. Come on, Rappaport, here's the main floor. Let's show this little crook he can't pull anythin' on our detail."

"Right," cried Rappaport manfully. They hustled me across the lobby while visitors gawked.

A boot landed in my backside and I was propelled through and ejected from the revolving door. I landed on my map on the concrete.

Firmly, and permanently, put out.

39

FEELING RATHER SULKY, I picked myself up from the horizontal and dusted off my Brooks sleeves. I straightened my crushed porkpie and marched down the drive.

That bum Celebreese was merely the last of a number of big, tough types who'd done me wrong in this little episode. I wasn't forgetting Gulf Bayles' surprisingly athletic attack. Nor the bullying of the blue boys. But even Celebreese's insults smarted less than the lightness of my wallet pocket. Of all the crimes perpetrated against my flesh, the heist was the one I couldn't tolerate at all. I meant to do something about it.

Rappaport and Warty, I saw, were back on guard at the elevators. That meant I'd have to try the trash can routine again, or some variation thereof. A rude disappointment awaited me when I reached the service courtyard.

Another officer was now stationed just inside the door. Emergency troops summoned by the other bulls? Probably. There was one more on duty at Emergency. Was my rep *that* bad? I shuddered, hurrying around the building and back to the boulevard.

Out of ideas, I studied the local landscape. I discerned the gleam of a candy store on the far side of the park. From a cabbie lounging in his vehicle I learned that the name of the hospital administrator was Dr. Casewit P. Carrington. This I filed away, in case my initial stratagem didn't work.

It didn't.

"Miss Wilde receives no incoming calls whatsoever. Sorree."

I gave the hospital operator the raspberry and hung up. I scrounged for another dime. I fed in the coin, cleared my throat. When another operator answered I snapped:

"Head nurse on the penthouse floor, please."

A moment later I got the broad I'd conversed with earlier. "Miss Blottworthy, penthouse supervisor speaking."

"Blottworthy? Carrington here."

"Who the—oh, Dr. *Carrington*. Oh yes, sir. Oh I'm sorry, sir. I didn't recognize your voice."

" 'S'all right," I muttered, to keep my words minimal. "Celebreese. Orderly."

"What? You wish to speak with Duncan Celebreese?"

"Right."

In a moment he was on, indolent and sneering. "This here's Celebreese."

"This here's—uh—this is Carrington. *Dr*. Carrington."

"Hey doc," he said casually. "Leave me call you back. I got a coupla body rubs waiting to sack out. Soon as I get the suckers settled in, I'll ring you up."

"Young man, you listen to me. We've received a very serious complaint about a sneak thief operating on your floor."

He was blankness itself. "That supposed to faze me?"

Bluffing wild, I hoped his history matched his viper looks. "Also, Mr. Celebreese, a matter has been brought to my attention. The matter of your—uh—police record."

"How'd you find out about that?"

"Never you mind."

"Jeez! It was only a coupla lousy hubcaps."

"According to you. Do you wish to keep your job or not?"

I almost fainted when he remarked, "Tell ya the truth, doc, I ain't sure."

"What? Of course you want to keep your job, man!"

Along the wire came an avaricious chuckle. I could just see his nasty little eyes glowing while he thought, *Hell, they pay me and I get the pickings of wallets and purses as a fringe benefit, so why fight it?* He assumed a more contrite tone.

"Yeah, doc, I guess I want to keep my job. For the time being anyway."

"Then we must have a conference immediately. Meet me at once."

"In your office?"

41

"Not unless you want the whole hospital to know. I suggest a private chat in—let's say—the park across the boulevard. Come out the front way. I'll be waiting for you near the first bench. And Celebreese—make it snappy."

He told me he would, then added, "But the park seems like a hell of a funny place for—"

"Never you mind, you whippersnapper," I cried. "Just be there!"

I hung up with a crash. My throat was raspy from the deep tones I'd been faking. I tottered out of the booth and dodged out into the wintry dark, wishing I'd brought a topcoat. I wanted my wallet more than I wanted comfort, however.

Near the appointed spot I paced up and down, rubbing my hands together. I was beginning to regret my cute little scheme. After all, Dunc outpointed me on weight, height and probably also in the extent of his liking for violence. But it was too late to do very much about that. Dunc's big hulk was shouldering through the revolving door.

He jogtrotted across the boulevard between cars. My natural cowardice took over and almost sent me climbing one of the bare trees. I tried to remember his insults, stature-wise, and stood my ground like a brave, if stupid, little soldier.

Big fists bunched in the pockets of his white pants, Dunc slowed down at the park entrance. I stood maybe a dozen yards inside the park, in obscure shadows, twiddling my thumbs nervously. How could I outguess him now that I'd lured him this far with my so-called wits?

"Carrington?" Dunc strode forward. "Doc Carrington?"

I stepped under a park lamp. "He sent me to conduct the interview, light-fingers."

Celebreese's viperish face became even more loathsome as recognition dawned.

"You! The little punk. You an' Carrington cooked up —no, wait a minute. I think I get the drift." He jammed his balled fists on his hips, rocked back on his Neolites and grinned a nasty grin. "That wasn't Carrington on

42

the horn, was it? That was you. I thought the voice sounded screwy."

Suddenly Dunc was handling both my lapels and nearly lifting me off the pavement.

"Listen, you little unprintable, unprintable, unprintable fink. What's the idea fakin' that call?"

I jerked free of his grip. "The idea is my Goddam wallet!"

One by one Dunc cracked his knuckles. He lowered his head and drew back his right paw.

"I'll give ya a wallet. A wallet made of knuckles."

He hurled that wicked right straight at my map. I ducked, bobbed back and aimed my head at his belly, determined to use butts, gouges and any other equalizing factors to prevent my own massacre. Before I reached him, I skidded to a halt.

Dunc's hand was frozen, half extended in the air. He was facing me but his head was screwed around almost ninety degrees. His jaw had practically unhinged.

I straightened up, puzzled. Then I saw he was staring at three perfectly ordinary types—at this distance anyway—who had paused under a streetlamp across the boulevard.

One of the trio pointed at the hospital's lights, raising his head as he did so.

"Jesus!" Dunc screamed loudly. "It's him!"

The heads of the trio snapped around. Another one pointed in our direction. They nodded, appeared to have a confab. I realized that Dunc and I were still standing in a pool of light thrown by a park lamp. Even from across the street Dunc's frame would be recognizable, especially in the white duds.

The boys bolted off the curb and headed our way. Dunc looked the color of a combination of ingredients tablet, chewing his lip and regretting with his expression the fact that he'd yelled loudly, involuntarily. He wheeled on me.

"Listen, mister. Let's get out of here."

"The hell with you. I want my wallet back."

The trio had reached the near curb, shoulder to shoulder like somewhat unholy musketeers. They kept putting their hands beneath their trench coats. That disturbed me

43

no end. Unless they were Siamese triplets they couldn't possibly have simulaneous itches or simultaneous urges for a smoke.

"Here, here!" Dunc yowled, pressing a wallet out of nowhere into my hand. He threw an arm across my shoulder. "I give it back, dint I, buddy? I apologize, old buddy. What's your name again?"

"Johnny Havoc. What's with the old buddy routine? Get your paws off me."

"You'n me, we're friends," Dunc squeaked.

I looked at the musketeers barreling along the park walk, then at Dunc. "You aren't getting any help from me, you miserable pickpocket."

The threesome came to a halt a few yards off. Unpleasant eyes gleamed beneath hat brims.

"That him?" one asked in a voice like Sakrete. "The big one?"

"Told you it was him when he hollered," replied the one in the middle, taller, with a kind of rum basso voice. They all began to sidle forward in a very sinister way. Only the lower half of each face was visible. Their teeth were nice and sanitary white, displayed in chilling grins.

Dunc jigged from foot to foot and chewed a hangnail. I tossed my wallet up, caught it, tipped my porkpie and started off in the other direction.

"So long, Dunc. Thanks for being so helpful."

"*You, little man.*"

Oh, mother. I shuddered to a halt.

"That's better."

"Whatever is going on, I'm just an old innocent bystander."

Dunc rushed me. I found myself in his embrace, being slapped like a lodge brother.

"Don't listen to him, fellas. This here's my pal. My good buddy Johnny."

"All right, Celebreese," intoned the rum basso, heading out forward of the others. "We got more things to do besides watch the Abbott and Costello bit."

The more I saw of this unearthly trio, the less I cared for them. Each little movement they made was quiet, professional. The three glided swiftly around Dunc and me, still with hands buried suggestively under their garments.

Idiot Dunc insisted on giggling. "How'd you find me, fellas?"

"We can find you," said the pug on the left. "We can always find you."

"Guys," I said, "I'm a stranger here myself—"

"Shut up," said rum basso, so bored I couldn't believe he was pulling out a large blued cannon. He concealed it from any observers on the boulevard by holding it close to his chest. He pointed it at my middle. "Just shut up, that's all I ask."

He pushed his hat back slightly, revealing a ridged, roughed-up and knobby face with mud eyes, a putty nose and a mouth that was a small, cruelly pursed O. He said to Dunc:

"We went inside the hospital looking for you. We checked with the nursie on your floor. Nursie was real nice. She told us you'd gone for a stroll in the park."

The sight of Dunc's craven posture would have satisfied me immensely in other, less trying circumstances. He whined, "Fellas, it's terrific to see you, really terrific. Came for a little talk, huh? Okay, sure. Let's all sit down on that bench over there and have a gabfest. Anything you want to say, why, say it right in front of my friend Johnny. Right, Johnny?"

"Wrong. I—"

The knobby-faced hood cut me off: "What we got to talk about, we don't talk about with anybody but you, kid."

"Goddam it," I shouted, "this punk is not my friend. He heisted my wallet and—"

Whappo!

The sap collided with the right side of my cheek, wielded by the hood on the right of the leader. I bucketed backwards to a bench. The wallet fell on the cement. I worked my jaw muscles. The chief hood wagged his cannon.

"Tsk-tsk, Myron. That was a little excessive."

"He's pretty free with smart answers," sulked Myron.

"That he is, Myron, that he is. Maybe you better go right ahead and insure our privacy with Celebreese by taking him out of action all the way."

45

Myron, the big lummox, was only too delighted. He lumbered in while the chief hood called to the third party, "For Godsakes get your cannon out, Lothar. Watch the kid so he doesn't take a powder on us."

Lothar obeyed, unveiling a howitzer-sized piece of armament. Dunc began to tremble at the sight of the thing. The noise unnerved the leader. With an exasperated sigh he snatched a sap from his own pocket with his free hand, and belted Dunc in the jaw.

As Dunc crumpled, the leader remarked wistfully, "You try and try to be just an ordinary businessman. But the jerks won't ever lectcha."

"Some business!" I said, trying to stand up. My legs were Jell-O. "Some damn business, walking into a park beating up perfect strangers."

Myron was practically on top of me, sap at the ready.

"Why, you're no stranger, little man. All of a sudden you're our friend too. We want to take you everyplace we go tonight."

His face twitched, a mask of dumb hamburger savagery. His sap arm flashed up. *We want to take you so you don't run tell the cops!*

While the blow was whistling at my conk, I leaped off the bench and let Myron have my index and middle fingers, V-shaped, in the eyeballs. He went "Yow*eee!*" and dropped his sap, capering like a vaudeville hoofer.

The chief and Lothar watched tensely, hamstrung by Dunc hanging unconscious between them.

I grabbed Myron's sap, whacked his wrist, then whacked it again, just to show the gunsel that the small guy, with the odds equalized, didn't have to be a permanent patsy. My temper was really up. Myron began to complain.

"Get the little monsta offa me, boss. He's killin—*oww!*"

Ker-thunk. That was a good one to Myron's nose. He managed to grab me with both hands. I blackjacked him on the back of the head. He cursed, hat falling off. He staggered to one knee, big fist reaching up to sideswipe my jaw as he went down.

Weak as it was, the punch rocked me. The sap slipped

46

through my fingers. I knuckled my eyes. The cement tilted. Knobby-face left Lothar to handle Dunc, raced over.

"Guess I ought to apologize, mister," he remarked. "You just kind of got invited in by accident. Oh, you dropped your wallet."

Fuzzy-brained, with my ears ringing like network chimes, I automatically glanced down. "That's funny, I don't see—"

The sap hidden behind Chief's back hit two times, three, across the nape of my neck.

Goodnight, all.

What happened next I prefer to forget as long as possible.

I woke up with my map pasted to the floormat of a speeding car. Lights flicked at the corners of my eyes. I swallowed, groaned, turned my head. And felt slightly sick.

A head lay near mine.

A head attached to a limp set of shoulders. A head with a very pale, a very unfunny and deflated face. The loose, sag-lipped face of somebody totally dead.

Dunc.

I think I yelled, a shocked, wild cry about that dead pitiful face. Somebody's foot massaged my ear. Then it came down a second time, harder still. What had started silly in a Santa suit was turning lethal. A sap hissed—

The fast car kept moving through the flickering streetlights. I didn't keep moving. I stayed behind in the black the sap brought.

Dreaming crazy dreams of Dunc's dead eyes.

Seven

STRANGE HOSPITAL THEY'RE running here, thought I, when the slits of my eyelids finally came unstuck. *All the nurses are out of uniform. Half out, anyway. Like the one bending over me this minute.*

A brunette beehive hairdo I couldn't imagine a floor superintendent sanctioning; a wickedly red mouth with

47

pounds of Revlon weighing it down; a sort of informal brocaded housecoat she hadn't worried about buttoning, so that the positively astonishing contents of her bra hung down in my face. Wow.

"Hi there," she said, ruffling my hair. She threw a guilty look over her shoulder at a closed door painted a vile chartreuse. *Funny damn color for a hospital,* I thought.

She bent closer. "I'm supposed to take care of you. See that you wake up. You look wide awake to me. My name's Vanessa. Gee, you're a little one."

Her phenomenal chest was practically mashing my map. "Nurse," I croaked, "what are you trying to do, give me a double hypo with those things?"

This set her to tittering. Without so much as a by-your-leave she crashed her entire self down on my prone person and gave me a large, long, moist kiss.

I writhed and flailed. There had popped into my slowly unfogging head an ugly memory of a face on a car floor-mat. A white, open-mouthed, dead face.

"Hands off!" I shouted. "Hands off before I biff you, broad—"

I dragged one fist from under her pulsating Maidenform to show her I meant it. Then I got a glimpse of the surroundings. Hospital, hell. The joint was a fancy, flouncy bedroom.

Vanessa climbed up on her fluffy mules, switched her plump tail and stared down at her multitudinous assets in dim-witted dismay. "What's the matter with me? Don't you like me?"

"Gobs. But where the hell am I? And what time is it?"

I looked at my watch. Ye gods. Ten past two in the afternoon, to judge by the light sifting through the closed drapes. They'd really anesthetized me with the saps.

"You must not like girls." Vanessa was pouting. "You must be unnatural or something."

"I'm very unnatural. I don't go for mattress antics right after I wake up, especially when the last thing I saw before I went to sleep was a corpse. Look out, I'm leaving."

She beat me in my lunge to the door. On the other side I heard a peculiar clickety-clacking. Vanessa slammed her back against the chartreuse panel, arms outspread.

48

"Get out of the way!"

She giggled. "I won't. I'm bigger than you are. That's what aroused my curiosity in the first place. With such a little guy it might be fun. Novel, too."

With my conk still smarting and aching I snarled, "Over my dead and totally unresponsive body." I raced for the window.

She didn't pursue. I hauled on the drape cords and rammed up the venetian blinds, planning to jump to the ground.

The ground was roughly twenty stories down.

Morosely I stared at the strange neighborhood of posh apartments. I began to get the willies for real.

"Whose place is this? Where are those thugs who scragged me? Dammit, woman—"

"Well, that's *something*," Vanessa said, advancing on me with her mammary glands at present arms. "At least you admit I'm a *girl*. I'm also a practically insatiable tigress. That's because I've been cooped up here so long."

Facing the possibility of an inglorious rape, which in other circumstances I might have enjoyed, I was being slowly backed against a chest of drawers when a voice cracked outside the door:

"Vanessa? The pigeon awake?"

She stamped a mule pettishly. "No, Polo."

"I am so! For God's sake come rescue me from this nymph."

The door swung inward. I didn't immediately respond to the faint tingle of alarm the name Polo had set off in my fuzzed thoughts. The entrant was the same knob-by-cheeked, mud-eyed thug who had led the shock troops in last night. He was nattily togged in loafers, beige slacks, a white shirt, silk throat scarf and a dark blazer with an Old Schoole crest that looked as natural on him as a girdle on Harry Truman.

Right behind him marched his two associates, the ugly horse-jawed Myron and the even uglier Lothar.

Chief made a thumb. "Haul it out, Vanessa. And keep the jugs covered, huhh? This is a business operation. I don't want you getting Lothar and Myron all excited."

"I'm excited," Myron whispered, owling me. "I'm excited because I wanna go to work on that little fink again. He's one of those smart aleck short guys."

Vanessa flaunted her overflowing cups. "I won't get out! This is my bedroom."

The chief snagged her wrist and gave her a nasty jerk that sailed her half into the other room.

"Your bedroom by invitation only, and don't you forget it! Now sit your butt down beside the ticker and call me if Consolidated Endless Belt drops an eighth of a point. Hear me? One eighth of point!"

"Ah, go play with your preferred options," Vanessa jeered. But she sat.

To my astonishment, I saw that the clackety-clicking piece of machinery reposing next to the stereo out there was, of all things, a private stock ticker. Chief closed the chartreuse door. I noticed a folder sticking from the side pocket of his blazer. The masthead screamed, *Dynamic Elasticity Forecast Theory Newsletter*.

That put some solidity behind the vague identification I'd been trying to make after my sex-happy nurse referred to him as Polo. A hood who fancies him a legit businessman? That would make his full name—

The bedside telephone rang. Chief leaped.

"Yeah, Hornbottle? What? Forty-*two*? Sell, sell for Godsakes! What about Golconda Unlimited Pitchblende? No bull? Buy, *buy*! Call me back, Hornbottle."

He hung up, massaged his hands in a satisfied way and squinted at me maliciously. "Like to do my bit for the American economy, y'know. Also makes a helluva good front."

"You also like to do your bit in reducing the labor force, don't you, Rogers?"

He let the meaning of my remark pass, and said proudly, "Oh, you know who I am, huh?"

"The stock speculator pose of Polo Rogers has been played up in the papers plenty. Along with the fact that you used to do the enforcing for Liam Sharkey, when he was still a live punk."

You'd think I'd insulted motherhood, the flag and cocker spaniels in a single breath. Lothar and Myron growled while Polo grabbed my already wrinkled lapels and crowded me prone on the bed.

50

"Don't speak nasty about Liam, crud. He was a big man. My pal. And I'm gonna do some enforcing on you, unless you flap your jaw the way I say."

I writhed and chopped ineffectually at his wrists. Polo laughed, let me go and stepped back. I bounded off the Beautyrest, red-mad and ready to paste him. I didn't when I saw Myron and Lothar casually unveil their cannons.

Polo sniggered again. "See, guys? He doesn't act so big and brave when he has to argue with lead."

Polo thumped me in the gub for emphasis. I took it, fuming though I was, because the sight of those lethal muzzles convinced me that my only means of escape from this bedroom death cell was fast talk.

"Let's not argue," I said, striving for politeness. "Let's talk about what's going on here."

Polo dipped his cauliflower head mockingly. "Okay by me, Havoc."

"How come you know my name?"

"The wallet, remember? The one you got back from that wise kid Celebreese. I also know a few more things about you. That you're a hustler. Got a lousy rep with the cops." A black, malicious humor lit his mud eyes. "Hell, if we weren't in this mess on opposite sides, I might respect you a lot."

"Try respecting me a little," I answered, in a somewhat conciliatory way. "Ask your pugs to hide the howitzers. They give me the jumps."

"Why should I?"

"Maybe we're not on opposite sides after all."

He digested this, scrutinized my fake grin, shrugged.

"I'd like to buy that, Havoc. I hear you really run rings around the bulls. But you were palsy with Celebreese. It looks bad."

"Easy to explain, Polo. I had some business at the hospital. It brought me in contact with Celebreese. He lifted my wallet. Light-fingered type. I was just retrieving the leather from him when you and your Olympic team arrived. That's my only reason in the world for associating with the poor kid who, I recall—" A cough, for emphasis. "—who I recall seeing on the floor of a car. He appeared very dead, Polo."

51

Ersatz sorrow broke out all over his knobby puss. "Oh. You seen him, huh?"

"I saw him," I corrected. "White. Ugly. And gone."

A sigh from Polo. "I thought I sapped you in time. Too bad. Well, guess that's all for you, Havoc. No point in gassing any more. Boys? Snap off the safeties and get to work."

"A pleasure," cried Myron. Lothar expressed similar sentiments. The cannons came out again.

"I hate blood," Polo explained, "except when it's absolutely necessary. Like now."

"Listen, Polo, this is damned unfair."

"Unfair unschmair. Your peepers are too sharp. So we gotta close 'em."

"Come back here! At least if you're intent on puncturing me, tell me why. What's it all about? Don't shuffle me off in ignorance."

Polo walked back. The pugs displayed dismay at the new delay. The enforcer said, "Y'know, I kinda like this little twerp. It takes plenty of hutzpah to stand up to the Sharkey team all by your lonesome. Have another weed, Havoc. By the time you finish it, I can tell you why we have to zero you out. It's simple, actually."

He licked his lips, the viciousness of the pro hood shining through his smile. "We want the guy that cooled Liam Sharkey. All of us. Me, every zone manager on the team. Coast to coast. It's a priority assignment."

"What's it got to do with me?" I asked. "I didn't cream him. I don't know who did. That lets me off the hook."

"Wrong. You were hangin' around with Celebreese. The little creep got in touch with the mob via the grapevine. Said he knew who stabbed Liam to death. Well, me and the boys came to talk to him last night. See what he knew. Actually I planned to dump both of you out of the car later. Alive. But while you were in dreamland, this Dunc kid— Christ, what a rotten bluffer he was!—wakes up. He tried to stiff me for a hundred G's in return for the name of the killer. Told me he'd deliver the goods in writing and I'd better not bump him because he had an accomplice on the deal."

A nasty light flashed in my addled dome. "That's not me. My wallet—"

52

"I know it's not you."

"You do?"

"He told me it wasn't." Polo shook his head in amazement. "Cheap threats. That's all I got outa him. A punk trying to blackmail Polo Rogers! Didn't know he was dealing with the top league. When I started to lean on him in the car, he caved in like a wet shopping bag. He got all weepy and hysterical—"

"Nearly wrecked the car," said Myron with homicidal relish.

Polo's next shrug was cold, casual. "By then I was convinced he was nothing but cheap guts and bluff. He didn't know the first thing about Liam's killer."

"That's your opinion."

"Okay, so it's my opinion, but it's the right one. I made up my mind he wasn't worth fooling with. So he hadda accident. Then you woke up and saw—what's the trouble?"

Covering quickly, I blathered, "Oh, nothing, nothing, Polo pal. I was just trying to visualize the situation, that's all."

Actually I'd visualized it in its grimmest aspects. My corpuscles had frozen at the use of the word *accomplice*. If Dunc Celebreese had an accomplice, could that accomplice have been Basil Todd?

The enforcer was still suspicious. I said, "How about leads? You must have some if you're so sure Celebreese was bluffing."

"Nah, nothing yet. But Liam always kept his private life separate from business. In fact you might say he was secretive about it. 'Course, one thing's obvious. It was a private kill. It had to be a private kill."

"Pretty positive of that, are you?"

"Very positive, Havoc. Liam was in perfect control of the organization. Unopposed. Either some deranged fink let him have it to gain a big rep, or one of his girl friends, like that broad in the other room. Say, I wonder what happened to Endless Belt—?"

The endless belt was operating inside my brain box. It carried me around past the corpse of Liam Sharkey to the sum of ten thousand green dollars being offered as a reward for his killer by the *Evening Trumpet*. All at once faith, hope and a minimum of courage were restored by the scent of loot.

When Polo returned from obtaining the latest querulous quotations from Vanessa, he suitably noted same on a folded-up chart from an inner pocket. I plied him with another careful, not-too-interested question:

"Did I hear you right, Polo? Vanessa was Sharkey's girl? Somehow I had the impression she was yours."

He sneered. "That dumb twist? Why, she doesn't even know what a capital reserve is. Sharkey liked 'em stupid, though. Stupid and athletic. She was one of his dames, yeah. We didn't know he was fooling with her until she showed up after the funeral, like she expected some sort of life insurance payoff. I been letting her hang around until we find who gave it to the boss. Well, that's the end of this installment of the continued story, Havoc. You won't make the scene for the next chapter. Too bad you hadda be caught in it, but we'll make it painless. Myron? Lothar? Got that?"

"Aw, *Jeez*, Polo," Lothar complained. "It's no fun if he don't scream and twitch a little."

"I wanted to shoot him through the calves a few times first," Myron said.

"Uh-uh. Right through the skull," said Polo matter-of-factly. "Quick and easy."

That chilling conversation sort of half floated through my brain, because out of the tangle of what Rogers had related, one thing made sense in a vague sort of way: the envelope Alfie was hunting.

Maybe Alfie had bumped Sharkey. Wanted to retrieve the envelope because it had his name, his guilt, written inside. Such information would explain Alfie's seriousness about his work. And Dunc's bluff, which I suspected was not really a bluff at all.

How it all revolved around my poor pal Basil and City Hospital was yet unclear, but the color of the ten grand reward from the *Trumpet* was shining and plain. If Alfie had bumped Sharkey, I guessed Dunc could have found out about it somehow. I wondered exactly how—

Myron grabbed my arm cheerily. "Let's go down to the sub-cellar, huh?"

Polo strolled to the phone to jingle up his broker. I

54

wrenched loose and hollered, "Rogers! Listen! I have a lead for you. I've been holding back. It wasn't just the wallet that took me to the hospital."

He snapped around, gave a signal for the gunsels to release me, then marched over and leered down.

"Little man, don't bull me. Never, never bull Polo Rogers."

"I wouldn't, I wouldn't!" I squeaked with plaintive sincerity. "I do have a lead to Sharkey's killer. That's how I make my living, hustling on tips like this. I got hold of the lead right after I learned the newspaper was offering ten thousand clams for information."

Polo smiled coldly. "The dopes. Those paper guys think Sharkey's murder is gonna trigger a gang war or something."

"Doesn't my lead change the situation?" I said.

"You bet it does."

"That's wonderful, Polo. I knew you'd see reason."

"We won't fry you downstairs. We'll do it here."

"What?"

He turned to his associates. "See if he's lying. Bash it out of him."

"Hot damn!" cried Myron. "Leave me roll up my sleeves—"

"Rogers!" I yelled, full in his down-turned face. "I'm getting mighty sick of being treated like some sort of federal agent." I switched tactics abruptly, put on a sly smile and hoped he couldn't hear the cowardly trip-hammering of my heart. "Look, I only strung you along to see whether you already had the information I do. Obviously you don't. Maybe we can deal."

"Okay," he said. "Who killed Liam?"

"I don't know for sure. I told you it's only a lead."

"Beat him up," Polo announced.

"Polo, Goddam it, I'm on your side! I *hate* the police. Grrr! *Poison!* All I want is that newspaper dough."

For a tense moment Polo tossed this latest statement around in his deficient mind. Then he squinted from under his hairy brows.

"Knowing your rep, Havoc, I can almost believe ya. Almost."

"Believe me all the way, Polo. You can send these

assassins down to the sub-cellar to work me over if you want, but I swear they'll get nothing out of me."

If he didn't choose to swallow that gobbet of bait, I was destined for a brief and painful future. All I had working in my favor was my less-than-perfect acting ability, and what Polo already knew of my past operations.

A tense second passed. Another.

"You could be bluffing, Havoc. Just like Celebreese."

"Sure, Polo, it's possible. But knowing how I make my kale do you think it's likely?"

"Suppose I take a chance. I want Liam's killer so bad I decided to play it the risky way. How do I do it?"

"You let me go."

He guffawed. "That's the most ridiculous thing I've heard since Hornbottle advised me to dump all my Amalgamated Hot Gas Valve. Incidentally, that's a swell buy right now at twenty—ah, skip it."

I seized his elbow, trying to impart a buddy-buddy feeling as I leered and whispered in my most conspiratorial way: "Polo old pal, it's not so funny as it sounds. You agree to let me have the *Trumpet* money and in return I'll slip you the killer's name. But *before* I go to the paper." *That* was a rotten fib, but I tried to keep the fact a secret. How I would doublecross him later was a problem for the future. Right now I pressed on:

"It'll be sort of a regrettable slip-up. Somebody chills the stabber before the police can latch onto him. I can't explain how they found out." I took a breath. "What do you say?"

A lazy, iodine-bottle grin lifted the corners of his mouth. I was suddenly sure I'd yapped myself into a dead end. From the other room came the funereal clicking of the latest flashes from Wall Street.

"I say," Polo said, "why not?"

I almost fainted with relief. Myron said, "Polo, he'll snitch on us."

"Oh, smarten up for Chrissake! Him snitch? If he romps down to the cops and tells 'em we fried Celebreese, they'll laugh till they cry. I told you I knew all about his reputation. The cops wouldn't believe him on a bet."

Wistfully I remained silent, forced to agree. On police blotters everywhere I was painted in far darker colors

56

of ink than I felt I deserved. But at least my shady side was—I hoped—going to pull me out of my current plight. Polo continued:

"Besides, Havoc's smart enough to know that if he squealed, it wouldn't do any good. I can alibi myself for last night a dozen times over."

"Oh, right, right!" I cried. "I'll bet you were out someplace playing cards, Polo."

"Nope. I was with Hornbottle. He's teaching a course on puts and calls."

While I was still dazzled by my victory, he grabbed me and folded up my suit front some more.

"If I let you go, I can still make some rules. Lothar, write down the phone number here and give it to him." A pregnant pause. "Okay, good. Havoc, you phone me within forty-eight hours. In forty-eight hours you have all the dope on who fried Sharkey. Or else the cops will receive an anonymous tip that the guy last seen with Celebreese was—you guessed it. You."

Then he gave me a push. While I stumbled all over my own toes, he laughed and added, "And what kind of an organization *you* got to provide an alibi, hustler?"

"Listen, Polo, I'm not sure I can wrap it up in forty-eight hours."

All he did was grin a mean grin. I glanced at Myron's weapon.

"I'll wrap it up in forty-eight hours," I said miserably.

The bedside phone jangled again. I stared morosely out the window, over the vistas of apartments sparkling in the chill December sun. Oh, Havoc, why were you born so larcenous and loose-lipped? What assurance did I have that within two scant days I could even begin to smoke out Sharkey's murderer? Only the lethal blue pieces of iron in the hands of Messrs. Myron and Lothar convinced me that I had no alternative but to try.

Polo took the phone and barked, "Hello?" He listened, turned white-on-white. He waved the Bell product wildly at his troops:

"You guys get him outa here! Ditch him downtown before I change my mind. Lava-Lava South Seas Motel Development just dropped ten points. What's that, Hornbottle? *Twenty* points? You no-good, earnings-doctoring, chart-juggling—" He turned aside again, howling, "Get the creepy midget *out* before I kill him." He pointed to me. "Just forty-eight hours, hustler. On the dot."

With kicks, gouges, jostles and other personal indignities, Lothar and Myron hustled me through the flat.

The bedroom door opened. Polo screamed, "Myron! Come back here a minute."

Lothar pushed me into the hallway of the ritzy apartment building. Myron rejoined us there a few seconds later. We whisked down in the elevator and out into the fresh, cold, alive December air. I was ghoulishly hungry, fiendishly thirsty and frantically thankful that once more my devious tongue had talked me out of trouble.

Or had it?

There was no absolute guarantee that Alfie, whoever and wherever he was, had been the one to fritz Sharkey with those strange neck stabs. In fact, the more I thought about it as Lothar drove and horsy-jawed Myron sat beside me in the rear seat of a big Lincoln, the less I could believe Alfie had anything to do with the killing. Didn't Alfie pride himself on his responses on the trigger of his pistola?

Then too, as Polo hinted, the queer stab wounds in Sharkey's throat, whatever their origin, weren't gangland-style death marks. Had a girl friend chilled him? Not Vanessa, I was sure. She was too stupid. And too smart to stay around if she had.

Who? He was secretive about his playmates, Polo told me. The more I pondered all the complications I'd jabbered myself into, the worse I felt.

The auto jerked to a stop on a downtown corner. Myron opened the door. I jumped with alacrity to the shopper-infested pavement. The car shot off.

Where should I start? I ambled along the pavement sunk in thought for about ten minutes. Then the short hairs on my neck lifted. I dodged in a doorway, peered out.

Dumb and determined, there was Myron halted at a light, tailing me.

He saw me, did a take, then lifted one hand in a mocking greeting. I broiled for a couple of seconds. Then I calmed down. When I thought of it now, Polo's release really had been too pat, too simple. Being tickled to escape with my skin whole, I hadn't questioned it overmuch right then. Now I understood why Polo had called Myron back to the bedchamber at the last minute:

Because he was a doublecrossing, untrusting, big fat crook.

Before I could set about unraveling the Sharkey knot, I had to guarantee myself some free movement. I had to ditch the clown.

I angled out among the shoppers. Carols pealed down from the lightpole loudspeakers. At the next corner I swiveled my head hopefully.

Phooie. Myron came on, like a bird dog.

I increased my pace, short legs pumping. In sixty seconds the chase was going full speed.

Eight

DUSK WAS SETTLING on the city, a cold twilight full of twinkling tiny lights and happy music and the shuffle, shuffle, shuffle of hundreds of thousands of feet beating up and down the pavements.

I decided to check Myron another time. Inadvertently I chose as my stopping point a patch of unoccupied sidewalk directly in front of the glass and steel monolith of Acme Thinking Machine Corp. There was Myron, half a block behind, pushing elbowing, gouging old ladies with parcels.

Quickly I lamped the crowded street. My best escape bet was to jayrun through the stalled autos, taxis and busses over to Osterwald's in the next block. Maybe I could lose my tail in the late-hour shopping crush.

As I pelted toward the curb the large clock on the face of the Acme Thinking Machine Corp. mechanically jumped its hand from 5:02 to 5:03. I was half way to the street when Acme's lobby disgorged the first six express elevator loads of its human thinking machines. All female.

59

"Ladies, ladies!" I cried. "Please let me through! I want to cross the street."

They'd worked all day and there was no stopping them. Employing busts and elbows for battering rams and talking like a barnyard full of neurotic hens, they fanned out to the left and right. An octopus pod of three dozen secretaries closed around me, pushing me back from the curb and down the sidewalk.

"Ladies, for pete's sake let me through! I want to reach—*lady*! You crushed my hat—"

So she had, the gray-haired female executive secretary type hurling along full tilt. She was a tall job, and carrying a parcel from the Frosting Castle Bakery. Because of her height and my lack of it, the box sideswiped my porkpie again and sent it skittering to the cement among hundreds of hurrying, clacking heels.

I took a breath and dove for the sidewalk.

A bright purple pump kicked the hat out of my reach.

I grabbed for it and accidentally hit some flesh.

A spike heel nailed my hand.

"Po*lice!*" a broad cried. "There's some kind of *peeker* on the *pave*ment!"

"Lady, *please,* you're standing on my knuckles. I only want my lid—"

"Give the masher the heel again, Thelma!" another dame advised. "Right in the butt."

"Disgraceful, that's what it is," said another hoarse voice.

"Oh yeah?" I cried hotly, strangling for air as I lurched up to the vertical like a submarine surfacing. "Look at this hat! Look at what they did to my ha*aaAWROOF!*"

Straightening up so suddenly that way, I'd neglected to notice that the dame who thought it was disgraceful was the same number whose pastry box had knocked off my porkpie in the first place. Just as I stood up, some vengeful sister shoved me from behind. I stumbled. My bared head sailed into the side of the Frosting Castle Bakery box, jamming it against the upholstered bosom of its carrier.

"Oh you dirty little *pusher!*" she exclaimed, swinging the crushed box. "You ruined my pineapple jelly *snails—*"

And she was determined to make me pay for it, by whamming me in the face with the box.

Frantically I ducked, sidestepped between a couple of cute secretaries with umbrellas. The box of pastries whipped through the air where my head had been—

—and unfortunately the Frosting Castle Bakery purchased cheap twine.

Which parted with a snap in the middle of the dame's swing.

I believe the principle is known as centrifugal force. Anyway, the box opened in midair and sprayed pineapple jelly snails like machine gun bullets. In a semicircle. Straight into the maps of pedestrians pushing along behind.

"*He* did it!" A female pointed a trembling glove.

Instantly two dozen pairs of mascaraed eyes swung my way. And the broad who pointed did so for an obvious reason. She had a facial layer of pineapple goo now.

Instantly I was the target from the dames nearest me. Handbags crumphed on my noggin. Spike heels tortured my shoe tips. Elbows abraded my ribs. Through this melee I said nothing more sensible than "Ouch!" and "Oww!", covering my head with my arms and trying to bull my way out, twisting and turning like a broken field runner.

Then I glimmed Myron back at the fringe of the group, struggling forward. Suddenly the blows raining on my backside slacked off. I was wondering why as I fended the jelly-flecked furies when my left foot contacted empty air behind me.

"*Yiiii!*"

I flailed for balance. Lights spun around. I grabbed for a rail, pulled myself up in time to prevent a fall all the way to the bottom of the subway stairs.

From below sounded the rumble of rush hour trains, a babble of voices. My side of the stairs was fairly clear going down. I turned and cut for it three steps at a time.

Four or five broads still dripping pastry filling charged after me. People ascending in a steady stream on the other side of the stairs looked on curiously.

"Get that man!"

"Get the F.B.I."

"He's a Communist anarchist dope fiend—"

A couple of paunchy executives were taking their sweet times reaching the bottom of the stairs. I belted between them and left them as a buffer between me and the jelly victims. I dodged to the right at the bottom of the steps, banged into a news kiosk and reached for a dime.

The area around the turnstiles was packed. The area beyond, where the trains hammered in and out, was even more crowded. I couldn't move fast enough to elude Myron in there. I had to try something really desperate.

The two executives collapsed against the wall, ashen, as the horde of outraged females thrust by. Meantime I'd bought a *Trumpet* and opened the tabloid-sized paper full width. With this screening my face, I worked my way into the press of subway passengers ascending to the street on the far side of the stairs.

Stumbling blind, I went upward, aware that others were rushing down just to my left. My nose was pressed so close to the newsprint I was unable to read anything except a boldface OODY RIOT IN SOU, over and over again.

OODY RIOT IN SOU, and up another step.

Voices complained behind me. Hurry, hurry. Some babe's girdle bumped my hat from the front.

OODY RIOT IN SOU, and everyone jawing about Cousin Mabel and what flight going home for the holidays and $3.98 in the Notions and how you made Tom and Jerry. All of a sudden a delicious breath of cold, auto-exhaust-suffused air crept over the top edge of the paper. I was almost to the top—

"Mind if I catch up on the news—*jerk*?"

Whippo, the *Trumpet* was snatched out of my hands. There was horsy Myron right opposite me, going down. In a trice he was behind me in my own line, pressing something iron and explosive through his pocket into my breech.

"What a creep," he laughed in my ear. "Think I couldn't spot that paper dodge? You're such a shrimp, you stand out like a sore thumb in any crowd. I'm gonna take you back to Polo an' tell him you tried to ditch—*where you goin'*?"

Into the other down line, that's where. I hurled myself

62

that way full force, right after I pinched the fanny of the dame ahead of me in the up line.

She whirled, a beeftrust with a mustache. She howled at Myron in such a giddy voice you'd think she actually enjoyed the pinch.

"Did *you* do that? Are *you* the one?"

"Oh, no, lady, I dint—" Myron began.

"I saw it," a man shouted. "They oughta lock these sex fiends up."

"Sex fiend, *sex* fiend!" a dozen voices exclaimed at once.

Instantly old Myron was absorbing the kind of blows with fists and pointed toes I'd taken on the street a few minutes ago.

"Oh Jeez, mister, I ain't no—I dint pinch her fat as—— I mean I never laid a hand on—watch them knitting needles, lady!"

I took advantage of the temporary stupefaction of the stair crowd to scuttle down again, insinuating myself between this body and that, whispering as I went: "There's a sex fiend up there. A sex fiend. *Nobody's* safe—"

Soon shrill shrieks echoed from top to bottom in the stairwell. Everybody was in a mad scurry to get ahead of everybody else. Because of my miniature size I had a slight advantage, scooting through this cranny between buttocks and hipbone, then that one. By the time I was two thirds of the way down to the platform, Myron was reeling and struggling to beat hell as the righteous citizenry closed in upon him.

Abruptly I had a clear field straight to the bottom.

But I no longer wished to go to the bottom.

There, pot-of-pansies hat awry, was one of the broads hit in the kisser with pineapple jelly snails. She was wagging whip-cream-smeared gloves under the red nose of an officer in a yellow slicker.

"—do something, *do* something! He's *somewhere* down here. Assaulting helpless citizens! Smearing up their clothes! Fighting! Brawling!"

The hapless bull protested, "Lady, there's a rhubarb on the stairs. I can't take time—"

"Aren't you a public servant? Go *after* the madman! He was cruel, vicious-looking. A natural born criminal type. Only about this high—"

She extended her gooey glove to measure the air and, in the act of measuring, spotted me coming down the stairs.

Her upper lip began to quake. "My God. *That's* the man—"

"Wife's got dinner on the stove," I exclaimed as I pelted ahead. "Coming through—"

"You! Hold up! Come back!" the cop ordered as I rushed around him and made for the first available turnstile.

The crowd at the barriers had thinned somewhat as express after express raced out, jammed with commuters. Once on a train and I'd be safe. Behind I heard the hysterical sounds of the fracas centering around Myron. The cop on my tail bellowed:

"Don't go another foot or I'll let you have it!"

Citizens on the far side of the turnstile turned to gawk. "Shoot and you'll hit innocent people!" I cried, reaching the turnstile and shinnying over, just as a subway system inspector who apparently had a spy post behind a pillar to catch slug-palmers collared me roughly.

"Say there, fella. I dint see you put any token in the slot."

"I'm a charity case, pops," I panted. "And your hat's the charity. Sorry."

The hat came off his head in one grab. I rammed it down on my scalp after shoving my porkpie in my pocket. I fended the inspector with my other hand, a difficult task since his reach was longer than mine.

"Gimme that, gimme that!" he shrieked. "You're impersonating a subway officer—"

The yellow-slickered cop and Miss Pineapple Jelly were waltzing around trying to decide who should go through the turnstile first. Meantime the subway minion almost had his mitts on my windwipe. I ducked under his reach.

"Where'd he go?"

I tapped him on the shoulder. As he turned I yanked a sack of groceries out of the arms of a fat lady and shoved the sack into his.

"Take off, pops," cried I, spinning him around again

64

and pushing him toward the cop who'd just pounded through the turnstile.

The dame from whom I'd filched the produce charged me like the cavalry. I darted behind a pillar. On the street stairway a regular donnybrook was in progress. I glimpsed Myron swinging freely and wildly. From down the subway tunnel came a mounting roar.

The cap! I still had it on my conk—

Miss Groceries rounded the pillar in hot pursuit. I dashed around the other side, cupped my hands around my mouth and bawled, "Keep back, folks, keep back! This next express goes through at 90 miles an hour!"

Irritable commuters mumbled and shuffled, showing little disposition to obey. I grabbed one guy and hollered, "Fella, do you want to be sucked under? *Here it comes!*"

"Get back, Hortense," somebody exclaimed. "We'll be sucked under—"

"Sucked under, sucked under!" rose the cry.

"Clear the trackside, clear the trackside!" I howled, racing up and down the line. All at once the folks got the message and began to stampede to the rear like a herd of upright buffalo.

"Quit shoving, jack."

"My God, we'll be sucked under—"

The cop battered at them: "Listen, I'm an officer of the Goddamned law and I'm trying to reach—awright, who's the wise guy? Who took the bullets out of my belt?"

The train rounded the bend and yowled to a halt.

Scores leaped off. I was the only one who got on, skinning through the doors just as they hissed shut.

The train began to pull out. I ditched the official cap, extracted my ruined porkpie from my pocket and had a last poignant glimpse of the cop in the slicker going under in a jolly fist fight. Then all I saw was a whizzing wall.

"Nobody got on back there," said a mystified straphanger at my elbow. "Nobody but you."

I gulped for air, swaying with the train. "They were all having too much fun."

"What was going on?"

"Oh, I gather there was some kind of nut loose."

I closed my eyes and shuddered as the train shot on down the tunnel. I didn't bother to add that it was moot how long the nut would remain loose, considering the kind of riot he/I had just incited.

Nine

AT THE NEXT subway station I detrained, along with several hundred other parties. On the platform I caught sight of my sorry, screwed-up suit in a candy counter shoplifter-catcher mirror. The banged porkpie was even more degrading, displaying several holes and a spot of pineapple jelly. I dumped its miserable remains in a refuse can and hurried up into the dark.

I shivered as I looked around. I didn't shiver so much because of the carnage I'd left behind, bad enough as that was, but because it was plain damned cold. The streets in this vicinity featured mostly large hotels, and were somewhat less gaudy and cheerful than those near Osterwald's where I'd dived below ground. But where there were hotels, there were bound to be warm, comforting, soothing booze parlors.

Shortly I was in the Olde Oake Grille of a large hostelry, drinking a vitamin refresher, double, on the rocks. The bar was quiet, refined. Even the plastic-cased boob tube above the backbar was tuned low.

I pinched the top of my nose and leaned my elbows wearily on the bar. I examined my watch. Criminey. Only fifteen until six? I felt like I'd lived through the burning of Rome twice.

As I was attacking my second belt the television lit up more brightly. Thoughtful engineers down at the studio hyped the volume so the consumers, who naturally didn't give a hang about the movie, could hear the commercial for which they'd all been waiting.

Weird Frankenstein music blared out.

The electronic bosom showed a stylized toy city block. On the dramatically lighted skyline there was a strange shape taking shape. The shape looked oddly familiar.

Half the buildings toppled over. The camera zoomed into focus on the head of a piece of mechanical plastic whose electric eyeballs were rotating furiously.

"*Kiddees!*" shrieked the invisible announcer, voice over screams of agony and the sound of masonry crashing. "Bar the doors! Lock the windows! Here he comes! The monster from outer space—Feend-O the Ferocious!"

"Gnargh, gnargh, gnargh," said Feend-O, knocking over the rest of the toy metropolis, swiveling his head and grasping here and there with his mechanical hands for some innocent neck to snap.

The scene dissolved. There was Feend-O standing placidly on a living room carpet, a couple of toothy juvenile Equity members hovering over, petting him and making goo sounds.

"Awww kids," the announcer chuckled patronizingly, "we all know Feend-O isn't that ferocious. He's your *pal*. He's your animated mechanical bodyguard. He walks back. He walks forward. He rolls his eyes and swivels his head just like a real live outer space demon."

More shots of the moppets putting Feend-O through his paces by twisting knobs on a small box. The announcer cried, "And there are *no* wires! Feend-O's sturdy styrene body is remote controlled, with wireless control power that reaches up to one-eighth of a mile. That's right, boys and girls, up to one eighth of a mile! *Wow!* Ever see such a swell Christmas toy?"

Many times, but I was damned if I'd ever seen one that was the duplicate of the creature Basil Todd had doodled on the napkin. That doodle was Feend-O and no mistake.

"—and here's the best part, kiddees," panted the unseen announcer breathlessly. "The price. For this two-feet, three-inch mechanical marvel a mere, a modest $49.95. That's all, kids, *only* $49.95. Now listen! Tell Santa to bring you Feend-O for sure—"

Another zoom, tight in on the brute's plastic fangs.

"—or you'll sic the *real* Feend-O on him. Tell ol' Santy that and see what happens Christmas morn! Feend-O the Ferocious! Another swell product of Titanic Toys Corp. Remember—"

67

You guessed it. A highly original firecracker animation effect.

"—every kid gets a *bang* out of a Titanic Toy!"

On this hysterical climax, the volume faded.

The bartender shook his head sadly. "Ain't it a crime? My boy Wilberforce beat his head against the Axminster last night until I practically promised him Santa'd bring Feend-O. Can't be worth much, all plastic and wires. Gettin' so I positively hate Christmas."

When I didn't offer an opinion on the subject, he strolled off. Bemused, I stared right through the television screen.

Basil's sketch showed the Feend-O toy on top of some sort of cart loaded with boxes.

What sort of cart?

Maybe—guessing now, but it fit—a department store cart?

All in a flash, I recalled Basil'd been running when he bolted into the Unicorn's Den. The bartender said so. The Den was located pretty close to Osterwald's and the other big department stores. In a tizzy I drained the rest of my hooch.

Now you don't suppose, I asked myself, Basil Todd stashed the envelope Alfie was hunting in some crazy place in a department store?

In a box, maybe?

In a box containing one genuine Feend-O the Ferocious?

Fantastic. Too far out.

But then, if I could believe Olive, Basil himself had been pretty far out that night. With fear.

I held off on the nutty box notion a sec, concentrating again on the envelope which seemed to be attracting so much attention from homicidal types. Did it really contain, as I'd postulated earlier, hot news about Liam Sharkey's killer? Such as his name? I could believe it, from the way Basil led to City Hospital, and City Hospital to Dunc Celebreese, and dead Dunc to Polo Rogers.

Okay, Havoc. You're progressing. Next step: that Feend-O box. Where is it?

Basil couldn't talk. Not tonight, not for several nights.

This immediately drew me to speculations on how Basil

had gotten mixed up in such a shady deal in the first place. I couldn't imagine him being so desperate for art school tuition that he'd stoop to—hold the freight.

Little Miss Wednesday had blurted out that she'd seen Gulf Bayles *talking* to Basil. Gulf and *somebody else*.

Dunc?

I was willing to bet on it.

I still had the sneaky feeling that Dunc hadn't been bluffing Polo; that Dunc really had an accomplice, as insurance. Do you suppose Dunc's accomplice could have been Gulf Bayles?

All right. Grant that. What reason would the deflowered Dixie bloom have for getting mixed up with crooks?

Failing theatrical vehicles? A sagging career? Lack of funds? Skidsville? It fitted, in a loose way. With Dunc and Gulf thrown into contact on the same hospital floor, and Basil too, it fitted even better.

Best method of checking would be to check Wednesday, even though that meant bracing the cops again.

Oh well. With what I'd done already, how much more trouble could I inherit? Besides, Wednesday had some tempting treasures that made a recheck very inviting.

Back to the main problem. How to locate the envelope?

Think slowly, Havoc. Slowly and carefully, about a cart full of Feend-Os the Ferociouses, if that's the plural, because the end reward of all this thinking may be ten lovely grand from the *Trumpet*. I did not need to remind myself that it also might include incarceration or a few lead pellets distributed throughout my person. I was still working within Polo Rogers' deadline, which was a couple of hours shy of forty-eight already.

A *cart* full of Feend-Os. What would a cart mean?

A new shipment unloaded?

Peacherino. How the hell did I find out who received new shipments of the toy that day?

Worse, how to check out all the people who might have purchased the toy around town? The total probably ran into the hundreds, considering how the commercials juiced the excitement of juvenile consumers to a phony fever pitch. It looked totally hopeless.

Maybe sleep would help. Put the subconscious to work.

I paid my tab with my dwindling cash reserve and said goodnight to the barman.

I loaded my carcass into a taxi and sat back for the ride to the parking lot near City Hospital. I reclaimed my heap, sat under the wheel a sec wondering whether to try Wednesday right now.

Not up to it. I still ached faintly from the sapping. I desired nothing so much as a change of clothes, another snort and slumber. I tooled home to my flat and saw no bulls lurking outside. I guessed they hadn't figured out yet who caused the revolution in the underground tube.

I dragged the bones up the stairs. In the dim hall I zipped out my key, was about to shove it in the Yale when I froze. My molars clicked in alarm.

Inside my dump, somebody was shuffling. Shuffling and shuffling. The description is furtively.

No thread of light leaked beneath the door. I tiptoed down the stairs and out into the night. Only when I was pushing my gas pedal along the cold, empty downtown boulevards did I relax.

I suspected I knew who was camped inside my joint: probably Polo's other fink Lothar, or a similar representative, staking me out. After what I'd done to Myron in the subway, I preferred not to antagonize my current visitor.

Depressed at the prospect of a night on the streets, I spied the front of an all-hours flick. I cruised by, grabbed a bite at a nearby hashhouse and walked a block to a U-wait cleaning machine joint. Customers sat in their Jockeys in freezing curtained cubicles while machines tumbled their outer-wear.

After running my Brooks through, I bought a ticket for the movie and settled down to snooze, uninterested in watching John Wayne make intense love to some cutie eighty years his junior.

Just before I dozed off I decided to go ahead and make a wild try on the morrow to turn up the Feend-O box. The box which just might have an envelope of negotiable dynamite stuck inside. After all, a guy can expend a hell of a lot of useless effort for the sake of ten thousand smackeroos.

Sometime after 6 A.M. I awoke. An usher was vacuuming the aisle of popcorn shells. Big John was still wiggling

70

his Technicolored eye bags suggestively up there on the screen. I tottered outside, wishing vaguely that I had the actor's physique.

Nonsense, Havoc, I thought. Don't you have a short man's only useful asset? Brains?

Debatable. If they were there, I hoped they'd keep functioning if the game got any rougher than it already was.

Ten

AFTER A NOURISIHNG coffee and Danish at a Nudick's stand, I buzzed into a drugstore, let my fingers do the walking through the Yellow pages and discovered that the executive offices and main plant of Titanic Toy Corp. were located right across the river in the smoggy precincts of Industrial Flats.

I leaped in my heap, tooled over the toll bridge and presently backed in the employee lot. An overweight receptionist told me the person I'd wish to see on the matter of tracing recent shipments was Mr. O. Leon Quimby, Vice President in Charge of Sales. I took the elevator to the third floor, entered a posh office and halted before the throne of a suspicious, hatchety old bag. A plastic plàque informed me her name was Miss Erdelatz.

I pulled myself to my full height and barked, "Havoc to see Quimby."

"Mr. Quimby is involved."

"So am I, lady." I flapped open my wallet and waved one of the isinglass envelopes under her snoot. The maneuver gave her only a fast glom at a flossily printed card. I buttoned the cardcase fastener and added darkly, "Investigation work. Drove all the way over from the city to check out a lead. Need Quimby's statement for a C.P.Q. report."

"Oh," she said reverently. "A C.P.Q. report. Like those police routine shows on TV?"

"Something like that." I neglected to tell her that C.P.Q. meant Call Polo Quickest.

71

She hesitated, doubtless speculating on exactly what it was she'd seen on that flashed card. The card bore my name, neatly typewritten, and could be mistaken in a moment of confusion for a police buzzer. I had been sitting on my pratt in my flat one night, guzzling beer, when a Police Benevolent Association solicitor, not knowing me by face or fame, called. Being rather liberally oiled, I had unwisely contributed twenty smackers. I never regretted the donation. It netted me by return mail the official-looking PBA membership card.

Miss Erdelatz depressed a cam. "I'll see whether Mr. Quimby can be disturbed."

"He'll be plenty disturbed if I have to make a second trip over here, lady."

"There's a policeman from the city to see you, sir. A detective in plain clothes. Something about—what *was* it about, officer?"

If she wanted to con herself into believing I was a blue boy, why should I disabuse her? "I'll tell Quimby, thanks."

"In there, officer."

"Thanks." I tipped a couple of fingers off my brow in salute and zipped through executive-type double doors into an office the size of an A & P.

"Miss Erdelatz said something about a police investigation."

"That's right," I said, snapping the isinglass under his nose too.

He did no more than grunt and fisheye the Benevolent pasteboard for the bare part of a second.

"Please make it snappy, officer. I have no time."

"Right. Like I told that old—that is, your secretary, I need some dope for my C.P.Q. form. We think there may be a significant connection between one of your toys and a recent homicide."

"What kind of connection?"

Lowering my voice, I let him have the full drama: "Mr. Quimby, do you know anything about the Liam Sharkey murder?"

"Sharkey? The hoodlum? Of course not! I'm in an honest business, man. What possible connection could there be between a Titanic product and Sharkey's death?"

I snapped, "That's confidential, I'm afraid. The inquiry is just routine. Part of our T.B.X. file down at Z.O.F."

"Oh," he said blankly. "I see."

On a memo pad I scribbled the date Basil took his lumps. "It pertains to this date, Mr. Quimby. Just a few days ago. We need your cooperation in ascertaining how many of your retail outlets in the city received fresh shipments of Feend-O the Ferocious on that particular date."

Instantly Quimby leaped to a file cabinet, yanked out a bulging folder, humming to himself in grisly joy.

"Won't be many, won't be many. That Feend-O is really moving. Literally jumping off the shelves into the arms of the poor parents. My son Flemyng had the idea. Drew a picture and said it looked like his mummy, the clever rascal. Let's see here. Monday, Tuesday, hmmm, hmmm. The demand for those automatic horrors is positively astonishing. We really manipulated the kids on that one. Hmmm, hmmm. Wednesday, Thurs—oh, that's last week. Here we are."

From the bowels of the folder he produced a computer-punched form, scanned it, then thrust the form at me.

"One store that day, officer. Only one. A shipment of one hundred. Osterwald's."

"How come only a hundred of those lous—those cute toys are sent out in one day if the whole country's clamoring?"

"Back order, back orders! Piled up to here. We've got the cash in the till from coast to coast, even though some of the tots won't get their Feend-Os until St. Patrick's Day. Of course," he confided, "by then Feend-O will be obsolete, passe. In the spring we'll be putting our big merchandising push behind Blast-O-Fun, the Backyard H-Bomb Kit with Harmless Play Fallout."

I stared at the meaningless electronically-punched pattern which Quimby apparently could read. I felt depressed. A mere hundred toys to check out. And Polo's forty-eight hour deadline nearly half shot already.

"Uh, thanks very much, Quimby. You've been a big help."

"Don't mention it." He was already riffling pie graphs.

"If you're a daddy yourself, just get out there and buy Titanic, hah hah."

Back into the vehicle, across the bridge and into a traffic tangle for the better part of an hour. Finally, in a Godawful temper, I managed to stash the wheels and battle my way into Osterwald's.

I soon wished fervently that I hadn't.

I'd totally forgotten that the schools had closed down for the holidays. In addition to the usual clutch of shoppers, the aisles were clogged with little lads and girlies in snow toggery. Passing each of these, I suppressed an hysterical urge to cry, "You've been brainwashed!"

Osterwald's was a mild treat to the eye and ear, though, bedecked with ten-foot Christmas trees, mammoth ornaments hanging from ceilings and salesgirls with sprigs of holly affixed holiday-fashion to their bustlines. The escalators up to the fourth—toys, bedspreads, Mightee-Kute Misses Shoppe—were six deep on every treadle.

The line outside Santa's Igloo, a clapboard and mica-dust affair in one corner of the toy department, was snaked back on itself eight times. Infants bawled. Lionels hooted. Erectors chuffed. A real din.

A harried help told me the toy department manager was Mr. Carpenter. He could be found in a cubicle that-away. If, added the help, he hadn't destroyed himself yet.

On the way to Carpenter's curtained cell I saw a stock boy pushing an empty cart that bore a generic resemblance to the one in Basil's napkin sketch. My hopes rose anew.

Inside the cubicle the noise was diminished not one whit. The manager at the desk was plainly no fuzzy-headed, single-track-mind number. He was a lean, sharp-jawed young guy. I tensed up. Though clearly in the last stages of mental distress, the manager nevertheless managed to cast me a Who-the-hell-are-you? glance while talking in the phone at the same time:

"Yes, Mrs. Wheeler-Whalen. No, Mrs. Wheeler-Whalen. That is not true, Mrs. Wheeler-Whalen. We are not giving preferential treatment to other customers and shipping them their orders of Babbling Betty dolls. Mrs. Wheeler-Whalen, I can't help it if you do call up your personal

74

friend, Mr. Osterwald. That won't get the shipment of Babbling Betty dolls here any quicker. No, definitely not. Babbling Betty will arrive any hour. We intend to ship one as soon as—Mrs. Wheeler-Whalen!" he practically cried. "I *can't* promise it by five o'clock even if your niece *is* being given a sedative by your physician. I can't help it if the commercials have got her so excited she— *what?*"

Mr. Carpenter climbed to his feet, turning cherry in the cheeks.

"You *do* that, Mrs. Wheeler-Whalen. In fact, I don't give a hang if you—same to you, lady! With mistletoe on it!"

Crash, down went the phone with a racket loud enough to reach the North Pole. He glared.

"What do you want?"

"Mr. Carpenter—"

"If you're one more outraged father going to give me hell because we don't have Babbling Betty, we don't—"

"Investigation, Mr. Carpenter," I cut in, flashing my Benevolent card. I had it back in my hip pocket while he was still craning his neck to see.

Wearily he sank down in his swivel. He peered at me through cracks between his fingers.

"You a cop?"

"You might say." I didn't tell him that if he did say, he'd be dead wrong. "It's a confidential matter, the nature of which I can't spell out too fully. I will tell you that it concerns the Liam Sharkey killing, odd as that sounds in a toy department."

"Nothing sounds odd in a toy department this time of year. Not flying mice, repelled gravity or nudist exhibitions. Nothing." He chewed at a nail. "My wife thinks I'm becoming unbalanced by the job. She may be right."

"I'll try to take as little of your time as possible, Mr. Carpenter," I said, perching my butt on the paper cluttered desk. "I just checked with the Titanic Toy people —relax, relax. Don't puff out your cheeks and roll your eyes that way. I didn't like those bozos much either. We're trying to learn who bought a shipment of one hundred Feend-Os the other day."

He reached for a drawer after I told him which day. "I

75

think I can tell you. We've only received one shipment of those worthless plastic gimcracks since Monday, and that shipment came the day you mentioned." He unveiled a sheaf of small handwritten snips of notebook paper, selected one batch held together by a shiny paper clip, and moved it to the center of the desk. "The master records are already up in accounts receivable. I hang onto these to have a record of my own."

"I hope too many of those orders aren't cash sales, Mr. Carpenter." If they were, I was dead.

"No, every last one's a charge." He flipped over several. "Charge, charge, charge. Shipped on prior orders. Weeks old, most of 'em."

"I, ah, wonder if I might have a look at that list, Mr. Carpenter."

So close. Oh, mother, so close to bonanza, and what does this harassed, embittered victim of parental wrath do but slap his palms lightly but firmly on top of the sheaf and say:

"Certainly. Right after you tell me your name, which you neglected to do. And show me that police identification again."

This was no time to fold the hand. I hopped off the desk and blustered, "Carpenter, are you insinuating there's something fishy about my questioning you?"

"I'm not insinuating anything! I'm just telling you that yesterday some fat clown marched in here posing as a county deputy sheriff and threatened to arrest me if I didn't produce a Feend-O for him on the spot. The Christmas season has made me cynical, mean, irascible, suspicious and a total son of a bitch. However, I will try to control all those tendencies and not punch you in the nose, officer, the way I want to punch any nose that sticks in here lately, and I'll gladly show you the list if you'll first show me your i.d."

The gulp in my throat was so loud he must have heard. But before I cut and ran, I was determined to bluff one last time. Snappo, out came the wallet. Snappo, open went the isinglass—

"There's the word police. Plain as day it says 'police.' "

"Let me hold that a second—"

I jerked the wallet back as he lunged. "What's got into you, Carpenter?"

"The funny notion that you're up to something."

Growing mad and desperate, I didn't pay too much mind to the exact amount of information I was giving out as I shouted, "Manager or no manager, that's a hell of an attitude to take toward a duly constituted investigator. My name's Havoc and my card clearly says 'police'—"

Carpenter leaned across the desk and snarled, "Benevolent Association."

"Oh," I said. "You saw that?"

"You bet I did. I'm going to ring up the store security people." He reached for the bell.

Thrust to desperate measures by the seriousness of the moment, I snatched the list from the desk, jammed it in my pocket and barreled out through the curtains.

I plunged down the nearest aisle, walking fast. Abruptly a frenzied voice rang out above the noise:

"Stop that man right there!"

It was Carpenter, natch. I walked faster.

"Floorwalker! *Somebody*! That little man's a thief—"

A floorwalker leaped for me.

"Which way to foundation garments?" I shrieked, grabbing his cutaway and hurling him around behind me into Carpenter's path.

Then I started running.

Eleven

"TRIP HIM, trip him!" exclaimed Carpenter as I navigated a circuitous course between several matrons and a counter full of Playskool goodies.

The toy department was so noisy, however, that even the manager's outraged bleat sounded much the same as the cries of parents calling for their tots not to break the merchandise. I whipped around the Playskool counter, dodged through a press at the glass-sided Lionel display, ignored the bug-eyed stares of a few curious customers and paused to decide which way to go.

77

Kittycorner on my right was a down escalator. But Carpenter was dispatching the wilted floorwalker to guard that escape hatch. Above the counters on my left glimmered the red glass of an exit stairway sign.

"Pardon me folks, pardon me, coming through."

I covered a couple of aisles, then screwed my head around to discover Carpenter in pursuit, joined now by two other floorwalkers whose carnations were fresh and whose thirst for blood was obvious. I pelted on, clearing the dollhouse counter at a semirun. Only a dozen feet to the exit stairs—

On which a porky party suddenly appeared.

I was half way to him, running like blazes, when the notion penetrated that the fatty in the unpressed suit was deliberately blocking the stairwell. Desperately I skidded to a stop and turned 180 degrees. The paunchy one was looking over my head, not a difficult feat, as if for instructions. They came floating through the air from behind:

"He's the one, Bagshot. Right there. Grab him!"

That lousy Carpenter! Porky fanned back the lapel of his blue-turned-green serge, flashed a gaudy badge.

"Bagshot, store security. Halt right there, mister. Oh, wanna play cute, huh? Okay, here I come."

In a wild lunge I snatched a two-room dollhouse off the counter and pitched it through the air. "Take this home to the kids, beefy!" And I was off like a shot to the right.

Bagshot caught the dollhouse like a football. He juggled it, turning the color of his suit, while I grabbed a couple of daddies in the Santa queue:

"That man's a shoplifter. Stop him!"

I shoved them both bodily at Bagshot, who couldn't see where he was stumbling because of the cardboard cottage in his arms. Carpenter and his floorwalkers chose this instant to burst into the aisle. There was a three way collision composed of Bagshot & Toy, the new reinforcements, and the pair of pops I'd propelled into the fray.

Up flew the dollhouse. Men cursed. Down came the dollhouse. Last I saw, Carpenter was sobbing and trying to extract his head from the combination living-dining room.

I shouldered through the first bend of the snaky line

78

outside Santa's igloo, then the second, the third, oblivious to the hot remarks from the waiting parents and the sobs of disillusionment from the assembled tots. I bashed my pate on the lintel of the igloo, a lumber affair, rushing inside.

Out in the toy department proper there were more ungentlemanly oaths, the sound of a general riot as toys were shattered and tempers too. A cute mother in a fox fur was standing by Santy's dais while the old fellow, an obese party with a rum-lover's schnozz above his angel's hair beard, dandled a preschooler on his red velvet knee.

I circled mommy and caught the little fellow in my arms. "Elmer! There you are! Daddy thought he'd lost his little lad for good—"

"What are you doing with my child?" Mama wailed. Santa tottered to his feet, catching an earful of the shouts, shrieks and howls just outside the igloo. Elmer battered at my ears and cried as I carried him to the igloo's exit. Just as I figured, Mama rushed in pursuit.

Santa gulped, hung an *Out to Lunch* placard on his throne and stumbled after us. "Gotta get a hooker. Knew I shouldn't of tried this job cold turkey. Fists in the eye, knees in the groin and now it's kidnaping—"

All at once the demoralized Claus was at my side, pushing, jamming, trying to escape through the same narrow exit Elmer and I were attempting to negotiate. A physical impossibility.

On the far side of the igloo, Carpenter, Bagshot and one floorwalker whose ascot elastic had snapped crashed inside one after another, knocking down half the doorway and making the lumber walls quake. I chose this moment to hurl Elmer into Santa's arms.

"Christmas present for the little mother," I panted, and darted outside.

Elmer's ferocious bawl, Mama's wistful sobs and Santa's delirious exclamations about taking the cold water cure created such chaos at the igloo exit that Carpenter and his troops were prisoned inside for the better part of half a minute. I sped down a cross aisle, moved through the next department at a cross-country walk, and patted my Brooks rig to make certain the list was still in the pocket.

Behind me, volcanic shudders and heaves shook the

walls of the Igloo. I leaped on the nearest escalator without even a first thought.

I discovered it was an Up escalator.

"Coming down, coming down," I cried, getting carried back up one step for every two I descended. The escalator seemed overpopulated with females who resented having their whalebone jammed against the side rail. But I was in a hurry.

"They let such common types in the stores these days, don't they, Margaret?"

"Outa my way, Mae West," I shouted, wedging to the rail. I had reached the point on the treadles where I could safely shinny over and jump down, thus avoiding the mob lined up at the entrance on the floor below. I jumped—

Smasho! Right into a salesgirl in perfumes. I landed behind her counter whilst she was demonstrating an atomizer to a silver-haired type in a homburg. At the impact, the girl's pinkies constricted on the bulb. A second later silver-haired Daddy smelled like a Spanish bordello, his map drenched with a quart of Libido # 26.

"Lovely scent, isn't it?" I gurgled, somewhat unhinged by all the madness. "I'll take two—"

I flashed out from the counter well as the salesperson began to shriek for help. But a couple of aisles later, I realized that I was on safer ground. I could slow down somewhat and resemble any other shopper hurrying along at breakneck clip.

Down another exit stairway, and I emerged in sporting goods. By various roundabout routes I reached the street level. I whisked through the revolving doors scant seconds ahead of a brace of obviously intent store cops come to seal off all the exits.

A passerby remarked, "That poor little man hasn't an overcoat. He'll catch his death."

Death, I thought. Liam Sharkey. Polo Rogers. The forty-eight hour deadline was half gone now.

Turning up the collar of my jacket, I hustled away from Osterwald's at a rapid clip. I walked eight blocks before I slowed down. I located a short order joint, sank into a stool with a cup of java and took out the rumpled, crumpled list I'd swiped from poor Carpenter.

My teeth chattered as I checked over the addresses of

80

the charge customers who'd been shipped the hundred Feend-Os. Most purchasers lived right here in the city, albeit in the suburban parts. Mercifully, only four were in the most distant suburbs past Industrial Flats on the other side of the river. I drained my java, ordered more.

And I was bulldozed by the realization that, even possessing the names, I'd have to be a superman to check out every last one in the time left.

As usual, my shifty brain supplied an answer. from a phone booth in back I telephoned the Holiday Bureau. When Nedrow came on the line, I asked him to wait for me at his place about six.

"Will it be to my financial pleasure to do so, Claudio?"

There was a hint of banditry in his question that I liked not a bit. Reluctantly I promised it would. He agreed to make the scene at six. I hung up.

Over one more cup of black poison, I laid out the sheets and began sorting them into batches of eight or ten names, according to location. One location had better be the right one, or I was cooked.

Six o'clock. I climbed the stairs clutching my lists. The Holiday Bureau was relatively quiet. Moe Nedrow sat at the counter.

"Say, Havoc. You look like hell."

"I look like hell because I feel like hell. I've been out in the cold all afternoon."

"We're all out in the cold, universally speaking."

"Spare me the philosophy."

"You said you wanted to talk to me relative to my financial pleasure. You never have told me what your line is, though. Or why you really turned up here in the first place."

"Didn't I say the guy who creamed you also beat up my friend Basil Todd?"

Spiritedly he poked his paunch with his thumb. "Who do you think you're talkin' to, some hick butter-n'-egg man from the sticks? I been hustling around long enough to know friendship is one thing and monetary matters another. You got that monetary look all over your map, Havoc, excuse my bluntness."

" 'S'all right. I'm too tired to argue. You're right. I am trying to make a buck."

"On that fateful note, I become cooperative."

Moe Nedrow carefully surveyed me with larceny in his blue eyes. "See the signs on the walls, Havoc? That's the key to the inscrutable Nedrow personality. 'Where are the apothecaries of yesteryear?' Obviously you don't know. Neither do I. But that's basic, Havoc. *Basic*."

I folded up my list. "Excuse me, I'm leaving. I think you're loony."

He grabbed my arm. "You want everybody to think and talk alike? Go to a funny farm."

"Maybe that's a point," I sighed. "But I can't be bothered finding out. Like I said, I'm trying to make a buck."

"So am I. And that's basic too. Get the drift now?"

"Vaguely."

"Are you trying to make this buck by honest methods?"

"Hell yes. It's a perfectly legit dodge. Just a little tricky, is all."

"You can't be a cop," he declared flatly. "Ergo, must be an eye. Lemme see your state license."

"Haven't got any. I'm no eye. Call me an exponent of the free enterprise system."

Nedrow slapped my shoulder in far too friendly fashion. Behind his sudden conviviality I was sure there lurked a large loss of profit for me. But he was my only hope, especially with the hands on my watch ticking away Polo's time limit.

"Tell me what you want, Havoc."

"I'm hot on the trail of quite a few simoleons, Nedrow. To gather in those simoleons, I need to check out some names on a list." I spread the papers on the dusty glass. "I have to do it tonight. Every last name, around a hundred in all. Got any unemployed actors in your file?"

"Scads. You know that, Claudio."

"I mean any who could be rounded up, say, in an hour?"

The highway robber gleam in his orbs intensified. "Might have. Illuminate me some more, Havoc."

"I want you to call up a dozen or so. I've divided the names into sections, according to where the people live. Believe it or not, these parties all bought a toy called Feend-O the Ferocious. At Osterwald's."

"I'm getting to like this. It's totally nuts."

"No, Moe, not totally. Inside one of the Feend-O boxes —I think—is an envelope. Probably so big." I measured air. "Somebody hid the envelope in one of those boxes and—"

Nedrow snapped his fingers. "Wait a minute, Claudio. That napkin you showed me. The doodles. Some kind of store cart. It had a sci-fic ugly riding on top—"

"Correct. That's Feend-O. I figure the envelope should still be in the box where it was hidden, because parents, not kids, bought all of these toys. The boxes are probably tucked in a closet or under a bed, unopened, waiting for Christmas eve. The guy who finds the right box brings it back here."

He speculated further, massaging his mop of graying hair. "Sounds simple enough on the surface. Some of the actors who sign up with me would go over Niagara in their birthday suit just to get work. But how about the ones who don't find an envelope? They'll want payola too."

"Naturally. Not as much as the big winner, though."

"Suppose I go along. How do we get the right box back from the folks who bought it?"

"Pay for it, for God's sake! Double the price. A hundred clams."

"And how do we talk the doting parents out of parting with such a treasure?"

I sighed again. "Nedrow, are these guys in your tin boxes actors or nitwits? Improvise!" I postured. "Hello, there. I'm Mr. Rumhenny, Titanic Toy Quality Control. We let some defective merchandise slip through. Must check your Feend-O. Reimburse you until we can replace the toy. Oh, naturally before Christmas." I took my paw out from under my lapel. "What else do I need to tell you? How to button your shirt?"

"Sounds okay. I guess I can have some fellows on the street in an hour. Provided," he leered, "*you* put up all the dough for their salaries and pay me a suitable booking agent's fee. Like ten percent on top of each salary."

"You lousy bandit!"

Nedrow guffawed. "Don't fake me, Havoc. I'm playing your very own game. I gotta nose for character. Yours is one kind and one kind only—crooked."

"Don't say that. It offends me. Say sinuous. But you're partly right."

"Well?" He squiggled up an eyebrow. "Deal?"

"On credit. I'm flat."

"On credit nothing."

"Dammit, Nedrow, I can't pay—"

"What's in the envelope?" he interrupted.

"None of your miserable business."

"Okay, Claudio," he said with an elaborate shrug. "You don't want that envelope that bad, that's your affair. Go out on stage and try playing your sonata all by yourself. As for me, your accompanist just quit. However—" His eyes narrowed slyly. "—if you spill, laddio, I just might finance the whole project out of my petty cash."

For a moment I masticated my lower lip, watching the little fives, tens and twenties flying from my bank account to his. Two things decided me. Plain old necessity, and the fact that I naturally take to a party right off, or I don't. To Nedrow I had, no doubt because in our dissimilar frames there coursed a similar off-brand of cockeyed, free-wheeling blood.

"All right. This is what's in the envelope—maybe. I can't guarantee it, I only have a strong hunch. The name of Liam Sharkey's killer."

Nedrow whistled. His eyeballs grew a brighter blue as I finished, "For that name, the *Evening Trumpet* is willing to cough up ten thousand iron soldiers. They believe Sharkey's cooling is about to touch off another gang war. It isn't, and it won't. I have that from reliable sources. It was a private kill. Nothing to do with the mobs. But that's no skin off us if the *Trumpet* wants to boost circulation."

"Ten thousand?" he panted. Then he harshened up: "I take half."

"*Half!* Why you nickel-stealing, unprincipled—"

"Half, Claudio. Else those file boxes remain forever closed."

Unaccountably, I felt like grinning. "Weasel! You're practically as good at hustling as I am."

"Laddio, in this case I'm better. Howzaboutit?"

"Okay, deal. As if I had a choice. Only listen—" I stabbed the air with my forefinger. "This isn't entirely a free ride, fat man. I want results. And I want 'em tonight. I want all your bodies to check in with you before

84

midnight. That means they'll have to hustle. I'll call you here at twelve sharp."

"Ordinarily I retire early with a fifth of champagne, but for five grand—okay."

"I'm off to City Hospital. Got a little suspicion I think Wednesday Wilde can confirm. Yep, I met her. Quite a dish. But this is busi—oh cripes. Me and my notions. I can't get back in that hospital."

Partially into his office and reaching for the files, Nedrow stopped. "Why not?"

"Coppers. At all the entrances. They've got my number by now. And my face on file. It's a long story, and gruesome. The gist is, I always rouse the ire of the police, and I roused it royally the other night when I called on Wednesday. Maybe I can phone—hell, that's no good either. I forgot she doesn't receive calls through the switchboard."

Nedrow bustled from behind the counter and plunged among the dingy racks of costumes. "I'll get you in, Havoc. Never let it be said that Nedrow let a partner flounder."

"Oh come off it," I snorted. He disappeared into the dingy nether regions of the loft, completely hidden by rows of costume racks which began to rattle and shiver with a grotesque life of their own. "Nedrow? Cut it out. You couldn't possibly have anything I could wear to get by the cops."

No answer. Under a sinister-looking work bulb huge clouds of moths fluttered up. "Hmmm, hmmm. Oh yeah, that's the ticket, that's the ticket." He emerged from the racks like a hurricane and threw a musty collection of items at my skull. "Hop into those while I fetch some shades from the office."

When he returned a moment later I was clad in a tent-like tan polo coat. I surveyed the spectacle in a flyspecked mirror.

"God, Nedrow, I look like I'm pregnant."

"Tighten the belt. Like this."

He gave a wrench that nearly gave me a hernia. He held up a pair of elevator shoes.

"I also found these Adler's. I keep a stock. Plus spirit gum, crepe hair in this cabinet."

"Nedrow, be serious, I can't—"

85

But he was determined I could. He grabbed bottles out of the cabinet and hustled me into a chair. When he finished with his manipulations a few minutes later, I had to admit he wasn't completely nutty. In the camel's hair coat, elevators, shades and a beret, plus an itchy Dali mustache pasted on my upper lip, I could pass a casual inspection and be taken for a Hollywood fruitcake.

"Terrific," Nedrow chortled. "I knew them Bastille Day berets would come in handy."

Against my better judgment, I reminded him I'd jingle at twelve, piled in my heap and hustled to City Hospital.

Cowardice almost overcame me as I entered the lobby. But then I recalled the stakes. I saluted the bull on guard by the elevator, the same wart-nosed specimen I'd tangled with before.

"Hi there, fella."

"Hi yourself, lollypop," he said, sour and disinterested. "Where do you think you're going?"

"Penthouse. Name's—uh—Phensterwalde. Producer. Colossal. Believe I'm on the In list?"

He garrumphed and threw me a hard look but didn't try to stop me. The elevator doors closed and I breathed with relief. My luck had changed. Upward I whisked, spirit gum, black glasses and all, for my reunion with Wednesday. My respect for Moe Nedrow had vastly increased, and my certainty of a payoff at midnight was now practically overwhelming.

Twelve

I SKULKED in the corridor near the open door of Wednesday's suite whilst one of the upholstered Flo Nightingales harangued the starlet inside:

"Really, you should follow Dr. Schermerhorn's orders, Miss, and take your tranquilizer."

Wednesday replied tartly.

Switching her foundation garment huffily, the nurse waltzed out of the room and down the darkened hallway to the main desk. I slipped out of the shadows beside the water fountain and darted inside.

I flung my seedy disguise piecemeal on the coat rack, pelted into the bedroom. "Hello there, doll."

Wednesday had been intent upon admiring a lithographed portrait of herself on the cover of *Scandalous Movie Revelations*. She was still refusing to follow hospital regulations: she was attired in a virtually nonexistent white nightie beneath which certain disturbing anatomical features thrust at the viewer with brash prominence. When she spied me, her double-barreled assets wiggled ecstatically and she squealed:

"The little man! Hello, lover."

"Getting pretty familiar, aren't we? And pretty noisy, too. Wait a sec."

I hustled back to shut the outer door. Wednesday laughed, "If you think that's familiar, just come here again." I left the door open half a foot for safety's sake.

At the bedside I attempted to sit down and narrowly avoided being caught in her clutch.

"Wednesday, don't do that. I'm back on business."

"Again?"

"Yes. And it's important."

"Of course it is," she giggled. "Let's go Bedsville, what do you say?"

"Much as I'd like to, uh, go Bedsville, doll, I really am here for other purposes."

She arched an eyebrow and teasingly began to fold back the covers. "We'll see."

"Such behavior."

She had the blanket peeled halfway off her juicy hips. The nightie successfully failed to cover those hips hardly at all. She made a move, shrugging. This naturally set the goodies a-jiggle and caused me difficulty in concentrating.

"Come here, little man."

I dodged around a cart. "Will you stop calling me little man?"

She paused, prettily outlined by the light from the bed lamp falling through her virtually invisible garment. "Johnny, I only meant it as a compliment."

87

"I'm not complimented. Guys are always handing me lumps because I'm short."

All at once she leaped, and there she was around my neck, wiggling and joggling, and nothing between me and total lack of interest in my work except 1/64 of an inch of white lace.

"I understand, darling," she purred. "I sympathize. Let me show you how much I sympathize—" She peppered my brow with feverish kisses and ground the goodies against my suit. "There. That shows you, doesn't it?"

"It practically demolishes me. Wednesday, let go because—"

"Won't. I've been thinking about you lots. Do you know how many men there are my size on the Coast? Not very many. Most of 'em are funny anyway. If you keep refusing and refusing, I'll think you're funny too."

"Wednesday, please stop hanging on me and let me get to the point of *smarf.*"

The kiss was pretty great, I'll tell you. It was obvious she'd done graduate study on the subject. I was a thoroughgoing wreck by the time she was finished manipulating my ears, and lapels. I came to my senses half sprawled on the sack, Wednesday on top and kissing to beat hell.

What a time to be offered such bounty! But there was no other course left open to me except diligent prying at her hands.

"I'm sorry, kiddo, I hate to break it up. Just let me explain what I'm after."

"I *know* what you're after."

"No you don't." I sneaked out from under her embrace, went across the bed on hands and knees, leaped to the floor and stood there panting while Wednesday glared. She flounced back in bed and covered her charms with the covers, all the way up to her shapely neck.

"All I wanted to do was give you a little Christmas present early," she pouted.

"It isn't Christmas yet. Besides, hon, I'm investigating, see? Trying to make a dollar for myself. It's necessary because I'm not in your class financially. Nobody's waiting to sign me to a lifetime contract." Except Polo, I thought.

"Now you're implying I'm a dirty snob."

"Phooie. I'm just telling you I came here for information, not athletics."

"Aren't you interested in athletics? Are you *funny*?"

"I am not funny. I think you're delectable. And I also have the problem of locating companions approximately my height. But I still have to bring up an unpleasant subject."

"What?"

"Murder."

Wednesday whipped out a comb and set about arranging her locks. "I'm thoroughly bored."

"Be bored, but listen. Do you know about Liam Sharkey?"

"What studio does he work for?"

"He's a hoodlum. Very dead. I think that musclebound fink Dunc knew something about his death."

Now a little frown-pucker disturbed her brow. "Dunc Celebreese? Say, I wonder where he's been lately?"

"I shudder to think."

"What does it mean?"

"Better you don't know. Wednesday, I also believe my friend Basil Todd, the artist who worked on this floor, was involved somehow in the Sharkey affair."

Her look was totally blank. I added, "Hon, give me a break. Don't freeze just because I took a raincheck. We'll play the game okay. But right now I have to stick to business. You said you knew Basil—?"

"I saw him around here a few times. So what, darling?"

"So just before your husband belted me in the mouth the other night—"

"I could have killed him, the slob."

"Let me finish. You told me then that you saw Gulf talking to Basil. And somebody else talking to him too." I drew a hopeful breath. "Was that other somebody Celebreese?"

"Sure."

"Hot damn."

"This is duller than a wardrobe fitting."

"Not to me, doll. It may win my fortune and save my life in the bargain."

Wednesday immediately latched onto my neck again and began wrestling me toward her munificent chest, sobbing, "Your life! Your *life*! Johnny, are you in danger? Is somebody trying to hurt you?"

"You," I cried as my neckbones gave an ominous crack. She released me, looking a shade more sympathetic. "That's better. I don't mean to exaggerate my position, Wednesday, but some pretty rough types are mixed up in this caper. However, I hope to settle the hash tonight and take myself out of danger." I grasped one of her small hands. "Believe me, I'd like nothing better than to romp, but I can't. Not until midnight, anyway."

"All right. Go ahead and ask questions. I'll be nice. I'll try to answer."

"Fine. First, where's Gulf?"

"I don't know."

"Have you seen him today?"

"Does it make any difference?"

"Yes. I'd like to get a few answers from him."

She frowned and shook her head. "Well, I haven't seen him since the other time, when he hit you in the teeth. 'Course, he's not really supposed to come up here at all."

"Would you say your husband and Dunc were pretty thick?"

She cocked her head. "That's funny, Johnny. The very first time Gulf came to visit me after I checked in here, he was hunting a handout. Boy, was I a sucker to marry him! Of course I was only eighteen—"

"Wednesday, don't change the subj—"

"—and he got me drunk on juleps and flew me to Mexico City from L. A. and before I woke up, bang, I was his Mrs. What a hangover I had! Still got it. I hope I won't after the divorce goes through. I'm just trying to explain, Johnny, that I'm not as one hundred percent bad as I'm painted."

"Okay, hon. I didn't believe so anyway. You were saying—?"

"That first time. I remember Gulf walked in. Hung up his coat on the rack in the next room, then staggered in

90

here looking like old mashed potatoes. He'd been on a long drunk. Of course he was on a long drunk almost the whole time we were married. Said if it was good enough for Edgar Allan Poe, it was good enough for him. Dunc was fooling around the outer room. Sweeping or something. I was so mad at Gulf I didn't pay much attention. Gulf tried for the handout. I said no. He stormed out. He grabbed his coat, then yelled that something was missing."

My brain sounded alarmed claxons. "Missing? What?"

"He didn't tell me. I was so sore I didn't ask."

"What happened next?"

"Gulf rushed out with wrath in his eye, hunting Dunc. That's the last I saw of him."

"You mean that time?"

"Yes."

"I don't see anything funny in that."

She tweaked my nose. "The funny part, darling, is that Gulf came back again next day. Oh, he was completely changed. Instead of pleading for a loan, telling me it was my wifely duty to help him till we were finally divorced, he started bragging that a lot of money would be coming his way soon. He didn't say what kind of money, or from where, but I know he couldn't have sold a play or anything. He hasn't written a line for a couple of years. Then Dunc walked in with my lunch. He and Gulf practically kissed each other. Doesn't that strike you as funny?"

"Certainly does," I said flatly, even though the picture was beginning to make woozy sense. "Think carefully, doll. Did you ever see Gulf and Dunc talking to Basil at the same time?"

She postured prettily, feigning concentration. "Yes. That very afternoon, right outside the hall door. I wish we could ask Gulf about it—"

"No dice there. He'd probably deny it. Wednesday, I think he's involved in this shady business too."

"Goodie! I hope they put him away for a thousand years. Johnny—"

"What?"

"I also hope you're not acting so reluctant because you consider me a married woman."

"Aren't you?"

"But Gulf's gone. Physically and practically legally too. I've helped you. Now it's your turn."

At the juncture I had two alternatives. Either continue to question her, when it was obvious she didn't know anything else. Or give in to my worst instincts and reward her for all her assistance. Being me, I chose the latter course.

Wednesday drew back, frowned. "Johnny. Why are you staring at my ear?"

"I'm not staring at your ear," I croaked feebly. "I'm staring at—at—at—"

"There he is!" exclaimed someone in the hall. *"By God we've got him this time!"*

I catapulted off the mattress. Wednesday uttered a low shriek. The hall door banged inward. Wet cigar working ferociously, spaniel eyes brimming with malicious satisfaction, Detective First Grade FitzHugh Goodpasture stalked in.

At his heels were the two cops I'd tangled with in the lobby the other time. Warty and Rappaport. Both grinned like ghouls.

FitzHugh planted his fists on his hips and glowered. "I'm surprised at you, Havoc. Playing Don Juan with what you have on your conscience. You're even more unscrupulous than I thought."

"Conscience?" I gargled. "Don Juan? What—what—what—"

"Don't give me that innocent routine!" He seized my arm in a painful grip. "Years and years I've waited. Now I've got you."

"What are you doing here? How—what—why—"

Goodpasture swiveled to the two uniform bulls. "See, men? He's blubbering like a baby. Shows you he's guilty, doesn't it? Finally got the goods on him."

He index-fingered me in the handkerchief pocket. "A couple of things fell into place, Havoc, when Officer Lemsdorfer here—" Hook of the thumb at Warty, who postured. "—filled his report about a punk with your name trying to crash the penthouse floor of City Hospital. We put this place under guard to prevent autograph hunters and other

92

lowlifes from entering. I happened to see Lemsdorfer's report. So I warned him to let me know if you showed up again. Because," FitzHugh finished triumphantly, "you are never up to any good wherever you go. Never, never, *never.*"

I muttered, "Guilty before I'm proved innocent. It's a dirty lie."

"Come off it, John! Sneaking in here in that hokey disguise I saw hanging on the rack out there? Beret? Sunglasses? Were you serious?"

"At the time," I replied. "I should have figured it wouldn't pass."

"It didn't," Officer Lemsdorfer crowed. "I seen through it right away, but instead of stoppin' you, I phoned up headquarters and got Detective Goodpasture to come right over."

FitzHugh rubbed his hands together. "And this time you're really in for it." He paused. "In a way, I'm really disappointed in you."

"Why? It was a crummy disguise. I admit it. But since when is it a crime to wear—"

FitzHugh began to shake his head mournfully.

"Not the disguise?"

He continued to shake his head.

"Uh—Fitz—then what?—"

"This afternoon we received an anonymous phone tip."

"Tip?" I swallowed, hardly able to pronounce the word. "Pertaining to—?"

"You, John. And to a corpse we found floating in the river this morning. We've been hunting you all day. No luck, until Lemsdorfer's sharp eyes—"

"Fitz," I cut in quietly. "Whose body?"

"Lad with a record. Name of Celebreeze."

Ever put your number ten down on the brake pedal of your vehicle and discover all the fluid has flown away and you're pumping nothing? That feeling is similar to the one I experienced at Goodpasture's remark. My shock was followed by mental apoplexy.

That bastard Polo Rogers had sold me out.

Tipped the cops with the forty-eight hour time limit only a little more than half gone. Why?

93

No answer.

FitzHugh shrugged. "Like I say, John. I'm disappointed. Confidence schemes, I expect from you. Twisting the law I expect. Not that I condone it. But killing—"

"I didn't chill him, Fitz. Dammit, I can dodge the rap."

"You'll have ample opportunity. From your cell."

Visions of restraining bars and impenetrable walls flashed through my mind. Wednesday began to sob and murmur that I hadn't done it. Well, I hadn't. That didn't prevent me from being locked up all night in the pokey.

And what about the vital meeting with Nedrow at midnight?

I had to be present, one way or another. Otherwise, if he located the envelope in one of the Feend-O boxes and that envelope contained any real hot stuff, being the highwayman he was, Nedrow would use the info himself. Trot to the *Trumpet,* claim the reward and cheerfully shuffle me out of my half of ten grand.

"Frankly, John," FitzHugh said, "I'm even harboring a hope that you can clear yourself of this charge."

"The bejasus you do. You hope I get creamed."

Goodpasture sighed. "Come along quietly." He took hold of my arm, to pull me into the darkened outer room. Officer Lemsdorfer and the other cop followed.

"Let me get my coat," I said, indicating the rack.

"Go ahead," said Fitz.

I took it down. "Help me with it," I said, and threw it at him.

"Johnny, don't make it worse!" Wednesday wailed.

Worse? Impossible. The polo coat had draped itself over FitzHugh's head. I kicked out to the rear like a mule. Officer Lemsdorfer was charging. He cried out in extreme anguish as my foot contacted his kneecap. He tumbled over and smashed Goodpasture against the plaster.

I sprinted for the door. Unfortunately the other lawdog now stood in front of it, and he had his cannon unholstered.

"Stand right there or I'll—*where is he?*"

I was bellyflopping to the floor and scuttling between his wide-braced legs, straight into the darkened hospital hallway, that's where I was.

Thirteen

THE ALARMS and outcries issuing from Wednesday's suite brought half the nursing staff pelting from the main desk.

As their white brogans slapped the vinyl I darted toward an exit stairway which I hoped led downward. The nurses let out shocked exclamations when they saw the bizarre scene taking place in the dim light around the doorway of Wednesday's quarters:

An unidentified person appeared to be having convulsions underneath a seedy polo coat, lashing and windmilling his arms. Two policemen were vainly attempting to subdue him, or so it appeared.

"Better do something," I informed the nurses. "That man's having a seizure."

"Forward, girls!" cried the head nurse. "Jane, you get the restraining sheets. Helen, bring a jacket. Send for the resident psychiatrist. These Hollywood people attract all sorts of mental cases—"

The mental case in question was indeed putting on a splendid performance. Officer Lemsdorfer tugged at him from one side, Officer Rappaport from the other. And the more FitzHugh attempted to extricate himself from the clinging coat, the more it seemed as though he was some sort of deranged party attacking both cops.

"Duly constituted officer of—" came his muffled cry. "Let go! Your fitness reports—Lemsdorfer, you're stepping on my *wowEE that hurts!*"

As the nurses fanned out for the funny farm equipment, the last one called to me, "Stick around, sir. We'll need statements from witnesses."

"Oh, I'll be right here," I replied, and promptly slammed through the stairway door.

The voices dwindled away:

"Calm down, sir. Just slip into this nice sport coat—"

"That's the way, sir. We're going to take you down to a nice electric hip bath, and then—"

"Goddam *mistake,* you idiots. *I'm* not crazy. That little man who was running around here—"

"Just calm down, calm *down.* I don't see any little man. You're overwrought—"

As I reached the next landing below, the closing of the pneumatic door on the penthouse floor mercifully masked the rest of the high-decibel debate. I got off the stairs two flights down and hustled to the elevator and thumbed the down button.

One by one the floors ticked off on the lighted panel. I perspired gallons. The fracas upstairs couldn't last indefinitely. As soon as Goodpasture squared himself—any minute now—I'd be in for it.

But the fates were on my side, the doublecrossers.

The lobby was no noisier than usual. I ankled my way outside into lightly falling snow. As the lady novelists say in their treacly prose, H.I.B.K.

Had I but known, I would have rushed back inside and let them capture me. At the moment, I merely congratulated myself on the narrow escape. I nearly stripped the gears in my heap driving away. By midnight, I kept thinking joyfully. By midnight!

By midnight Nedrow will have the goods and all will be well.

By midnight, I can start planning on how to square up with Goodpasture.

By midnight I'll have the money I need to pay my bills.

As it turned out, by midnight the mayhem was only beginning.

Since I had considerable time at my disposal, I decided against visiting restaurants, bars and other public watering places. I contented myself with cruising around through the slush while the hours went slowly by. Ten times around the park couldn't have been duller, but at least I was safe in my own wagon.

The hands on the dash clock inched and inched. I whistled with relief when at last they stood at five until twelve.

The snow slacked off. I cruised into an all-night filling station. I told the attendant to fill her up and went into the station building.

With somewhat shaky fingers I dialed the Holiday Bureau. Nedrow seemed to take a long time answering.

At last the receiver clicked. "We're closed for the night."

"Better not be closed, you bandit," I whispered. "This is J. H. Got the goods?"

"Have I, Claudio!"

"You don't sound very happy about it."

"I'm not. But I've got the envelope and the Feend-O box. It was right under the bed of Mr. and Mrs.—lemme see here a sec, I wrote it down—Frampton Hillingsbee, Scenic Lane, out in—"

"You can omit the geography. No doubt you've read the contents already."

"Wow, you bet. Hot stuff."

"Give me a quick rundown before—oh, cripes. Hang on a second."

The gas monkey sauntered into the station. "Fo' dollars ten cents."

"Okay, okay, right with you." I cupped the phone close. Before I could speak, I noticed a police prowl car crawling by the station. Routine? I didn't know, but it gave me the willies. "Listen, Nedrow, I'd better not talk any more now. Meet me right away at Manny's Gastric Heaven. No, Goddam it, that's not a gag. It's a twenty-four hour diner just down the block from my place. No, I haven't got time to give you the address. Look it up. And bring the merchandise."

I hung up. I fumbled for money to pay for the ethyl, watched the prowl boat turn the corner and roll out of sight. Routine after all. But the effect on my ticker hadn't been routine. It was thumping a mile a minute.

Back in my heap, I drove downtown in the general direction of my digs. I wondered whether the spur-of-the-moment decision to meet Nedrow near my own home grounds was wise.

But the more I thought about it, the more sensible it seemed. FitzHugh Goodpasture would probably have my place staked out pretty soon, if he didn't already. And Nedrow had the goods. With luck, we could wrap it up quickly—

Provided the material in the envelope actually named Liam Sharkey's killer.

Granted it did, Nedrow and I could simply scurry across the street, locate the police FitzHugh had put on stakeout, and surrender the envelope to them. The ten grand reward, splitable, would follow in due course.

I also thought I knew a way of earning some bonus points. Perhaps I could even mollify the good Detective First Grade. The previous night I'd heard somebody pussy-footing in my joint. One of Polo's hoods, I was sure.

There was a slim chance he might be waiting there still. I had no idea why Polo had screwed me up by phoning the bulls about Dunc, though I didn't doubt he was the guilty party. Maybe he thought that by driving me north—on the lam, so to speak—I'd run south, into his helpful arms, and would spill what I knew. Maybe that was why he'd assigned a trooper to my diggings.

Anyway, it was worth the effort to tell FitzHugh's men that a representative of the crook who killed Dunc might be lurking in my apartment.

If the police barged in and Polo's clown had fled, what was the harm? But if he was still on the premises, Fitz might count it an extra score in his favor. And mine, thereby modifying his demands for my neck on the penal guillotine.

Nothing like playing all the angles. Considering my rep, there was hardly another choice. With a jolt I saw I was nearing my own neighborhood.

Once or twice in the past, when I ran out of TV dinners, I had been forced to drop in at Manny's Gastric Heaven for a meal, an experience my duodenum preferred to forget. It was a long, low joint, built in the days when railroad car eateries were all the rage. Gearing down, I tooled past. I saw nobody inside except a counterman.

Then I got a worse shock.

Usually police types on stakeout are as obvious as cauliflower ears. But the curb in front of my building was empty of suspicious vehicles. I saw no doorway lurkers. In fact, nobody. Snow drifting down past the black, blank windows of my apartment was silent, eerie. There was a tomblike stillness about the scene that made me more nervous than ever.

I U-turned, parked a block from my building, then hurried back along the shining sidewalk with my collar turned up and snow prickling my scalp. The wind was rising. I wished my porkpie hadn't been demolished. I wished I was in Bali-Bali on the beach. I wished a lot of things, all having to do with my own safety.

Why, oh why did I have to be born with such a larcenous brain? A brain which pushed me into cold, lonesome, ominous situations like this one?

Imagination, Havoc! There's nobody around. The street was still quiet, except for a solitary drunk who'd just stumbled into the cone of light thrown by a lamp post at the corner beyond Gastric Heaven.

I slid into the doorway of G.H. and watched the drunk. He was a black outline, tottering unsteadily. The drunk was a drunk, not a cop. I have a weird talent for spotting cops. And they have no acting ability, generally. Reassured, I shoved inside.

The counterman was immersed in the latest issue of a girlie publication. He closed a gatefold view of some bim's Technicolored cleavage and inquired as to what I would have.

"Two cups of java and some privacy."

He yawned. "Two cups?"

"I'm expecting a friend. Then go read your flesh book in the kitchen, okay?"

He served up the black brew, some of whch I downed hurriedly. I'd never known before that it was possible to scorch coffee. I lit a weed and waited. Presently a taxi buzzed along the street, pulled up outside.

The door gusted open. Wind whistled. I jumped up.

"Don't fly through the plaster," Nedrow panted. " 'S'only me."

Furtively he slid onto the stool next to mine. The taxi drove away. I shoved over the lukewarm coffee. "No thanks," he said, looking harassed and not quite so sure of himself as he'd been earlier. Flakes sparkled in his mop of graying hair and melted on a big brown paper sack which he laid on the counter.

The master chef peered at us from a serving slit in the

kitchen. I jerked my thumb. He blushed and dodged out of sight.

I stared greedily at the end of the gayly printed carton protruding from the sack.

"Open it, Moe. Do the honors."

"Yeah, yeah, sure." He glanced out the window. His pinkies shook.

"What's wrong with you?"

"I got the jumps, Claudio."

"Drink your coffee."

He did so, slurping. I pried at the flap of the box which bore the legend *Feend-O the Ferocious*. Inside the toy crate, the top of the monster's green plastic pate protruded through a diecut bracing piece of heavy brown corrugated. Wedged in between this piece and the box wall was a rumpled envelope.

"Manna," I said, pulling it out. "This is really the goods?"

"The goods. Havoc, I'm kinda sorry I got into this. I'm not the dying type."

"Who's going to die? We're perfectly safe."

"I dunno about that. We're in with some rough company. Wait till you read—"

"Shut up and let me," I interrupted, opening the envelope.

Nedrow continued to glance balefully out the windows. There was nary a noise nor disturbance except the ticking of the downy stuff against the glass. Three single-spaced typewritten sheets popped onto the formica, together with a smaller piece, hand-written in an unfamiliar scrawl.

The note announced that the supression of all "future copies" of the typewritten material would cost fifty thousand dollars.

"I see what you mean," I said. "This isn't penny ante."

"Hurry up and finish. Then let's go to the police, quick."

"Wait, wait," I said, reading the top line aloud. " *This is a little tale about what happened in a miserable Yankee city where the winters are cold but the immutably dead remains of a certain man are colder.'* "

I blinked. "Yankee city? Cold winters? If that's not

Gulf Bayles or somebody imitating him, then I'm an extinct dodo."

Nedrow merely stared at me unhappily. I turned back to the paragraphed prose, gasping as I read on.

Written in narrative style, much like a limp and wispy short story, it was the damndest account of murder you ever read. All in the first person. Lots of vague allusions to classical myths. Full of introspective maunderings. But containing a grimly discernible plot none the less.

The overwrought *"I"* identified himself as a gent down on his luck. The opening section described how he went on an extended booze binge, *"tottering through the concretized effluvium of Northern indifference in a wild search for scented yesterdays."*

He wound up at a club to which he belonged, sleeping it off behind a low, wide sofa in an alcove in one of the club's flossy private dining rooms. Here the style changed to flat declaratives that knocked me right between the optical pieces:

"The name of that club was The Aphrodite."

Nedrow had finished with his coffee. "Got to the murder yet?"

"No. Stop interrupting."

The nameless *"I"* woke up with an aching cranium and discovered that a man and woman were having dinner alone in the room. And didn't know he'd been sleeping behind the divan for hours and hours.

Petrified, *"I"* lay still. The man and woman were arguing like hell over the guy's new girl friend. A chick named—my God—Vanessa.

Not knowing what to do, our shrinking author continued to recline, terrified, wedged next to the baseboard out of sight. The argument got hotter. The broad was jealous. She grew hysterical. Then the man slapped her.

Then she let the man have it right through the throat. With a fork.

"The stab wounds! The funny stab wounds in Sharkey's throat!"

Nedrow didn't even glance up. He was chewing a hangnail ferociously.

In the next paragraph the author heard the dame leave

101

the room. The author thereupon decided to get the hell out. The dining room was awash with blood, and Sharkey made a hideous sight with the utensil in his neck. But before our nervous hero could make it to the corridor, he heard the woman returning, accompanied by another man. Author then rushes back to the sofa, hides, but manages to sneak a peek at the new arrival.

I read the man's description and began to understand why Nedrow had the jimjams.

The description fit Alfie, perfectly.

The woman and Alfie carried the body out. In that interval *"I"* managed to escape, fleeing down a back service stairs. He knew now—and spelled it out in the typewriting—that Miss Ina Young had been one of Liam Sharkey's dollfriends, and had murdered him.

"Ina Young!" I breathed to myself. "I completely crossed her off. Why, she must have lied to me with that story of Basil looking for a mural job. He probably delivered the blackmail package, got scared and hightailed."

Nedrow jumped up. "Done?"

"Yes, but—"

"Let's blow to the local precinct. I'm nervous."

"One more second, Moe. It's falling together. Dunc and Gulf must have been using Basil as go-between. Maybe Dunc was trying to play both ends at once."

Then a puzzle reared up. How had Alfie known Basil was to play Santa on that streetcorner that night? Alfie found me instead, and—

"Havoc, please. Let's get outa here."

"All right. You're making me nervous too." I peered out the window. No sign of police anywhere. "On second thought, let's not take any unnecessary risks. This place is warm and well-lighted. Let's just camp and I'll phone the cops from here."

I started down the counter toward a pay phone on the wall. The front door burst open.

A big man bulked there, his overcoat shoulders gleaming with snow crystals. His eyes gleamed with homicide. And so did the muzzle of the cannon in his right paw.

"Hiyah," said Alfie.

Fourteen

"HIM," Moe Nedrow gargled, turning the hue of flour. "Hi-hi-hi-*him*."

"Well, it ain't Saint Nick hoistin' his belly down the chimney, that's for sure," said Alfie, leaning against the door frame.

I debated trying to jump him. Alfie's cold, narrow face jerked in grim mirth.

"I see what you're thinking, wart. Remember those fast reflexes I mentioned the first time we met. Don't set 'em off unless your hospitalization's paid up."

So there I stood like a slab of wood. Nedrow breathed louder than a steam engine. Alfie shifted his weight, flicked snow off the collar of his cashmere overcoat. The rod was held in close to his ribs. Any unimaginative soul passing on the pavement would see the scene through the windows as a harmless conversation between three people.

"I didn't bargain for this kind of woe, Claudio," Nedrow burbled.

"How'd you like to lose five pounds, lardy?" Alfie said. "I got something better than Metrecal in this cannon. One more yap and we'll start the reducing treatment."

"Say, what in the fire's going on—oh, gollies," said the lamebrain counterman, drawn from the kitchen by Nedrow's agitated outcry. The man froze behind a platter of doughnuts on the counter.

Alfie brandished his firearm. "Go back inside."

"Let's not have no trouble, mister," the idiot whined. "Manny'll kill me if the place is messed up. You go on, get out of here!"

Where the counterman got his courage, I couldn't imagine, unless it was from the same defective place he got his brains. As the poor wretch started to badger Alfie again, the gunman lammed the poor wretch in the skull with the rod. The counterman folded behind the counter.

"Stand still," Alfie warned me, leaping around to crouch over his victim. Idiot Moe crowded close to my side instead of staying where he was, thus providing Alfie with a convenient single target.

One-handed, Alfie stuffed the counterman's jaw full of paper napkins, then bound the gag in place with a dish towel he managed to knot using only five fingers. I sneaked a look out the window.

Not a sign of anybody, anywhere.

Where in dingdong hell were FitzHugh's cops?

"That does it," Alfie grunted, rising. "You two jokers sit down while I make things more private."

Moving swiftly, he jerked the window blind cords one after another. The slats dropped over the panes and hid us from any and all help. I sat down on a stool. Cold sweat bathed me, head to foot. Nedrow clutched the Feend-O box like a prized possession. He stared at Alfie in a glazed, cross-eyed way. I hoped the poor bandit didn't crack.

Alfie menaced him. "Hear what I said, fatty? I dunno why you're in this deal, but I'll take you out of it in three seconds if you don't mind your manners. *Sit down.*"

Nedrow sat. "I can't stand this. I'm very fragile, nerve-wise."

Alfie strolled to the door, flipped the *Closed* sign around, drew the shade. Then he walked behind the counter. He kept the heater leveled while he munched a couple of doughnuts from the plate.

"I was planning to cream you both when you walked outside," he announced cheerily.

"How long have you been standing out there?" I asked.

"Long enough. I saw you drive up, Havoc. I played drunk."

"You were the one reeling around down on the corner?"

"Who'd you think it was? Ray Milland?"

"Somebody like that."

Alfie sniggered at my stupidity, explained, "I came over here hunting for you, shrimp. Before I got to your place I saw you arrive in the heap. So I went into the plastered routine to see what was up. Like I said, I figured on pumping you full when you walked out. But the minute you headed for that wall phone, my reflexes told me, Alfie baby, get going before wiseguy makes any kind of call."

He brushed confectioner's sugar off his chin, waiting to see my reaction. Ordinarily I would have given vent to my true feelings—rampant cowardice—and babbled for mercy. But it was plain Alfie wasn't going to be merciful. Especially not with those three typed pages and the note still reposing in plain sight between empty coffee cups. So I called on what few reserves of histrionic ability I had left, said with fake nonchalance:

"I suppose you came for that little story right there."

Alfie nodded. He crushed the papers into a ball, shoved the ball into the side pocket of the cashmere coat.

"And now I got it. So there we are."

"Who sent you? Ina Young?"

"As if you didn't know."

A tiny suspicious seed in my dome ripened in seconds. Did the gunsel and his murdering mistress really know who authored that stuff? With all my face muscles at rigid attention I waved.

"I don't get you, Alfie."

"For Christ's sake! How stupid do you think we are? You wrote that stuff."

"I won't deny that, Alfie."

He beamed.

"I won't admit I did, either."

He scowled, uncertain.

Meantime, Nedrow was rocking back and forth on his stool, lovingly clasping Feend-O and mumbling that he should have gone into some safer line, such as skin diving without any aqua lung. All at once I had a faint glimmer about a tricky way out of this fatal bind. If only Moe wouldn't cross me up—or send Alfie hair-triggering off.

"Calm down, Moe," I said, slapping his arm. "Hear me, Moe? Take it easy! No sweat! Let him take the papers, and good riddance. Can I ask you a question, Alfie? Just one?"

"Don't see why not. I got the situation under control."

"How come you're after me tonight all of a sudden?"

"Simple, simpleton. My boss, Miss Young, decided that when you came to the club to ask about that dumbhead Todd, the question was legit. And you were harmless. You didn't know a blessed thing."

"She was right. I didn't know anything, then."

"Miss Young got rid of you. Forgot about you, even though we'd already tangled on the street. I wanted to meet you one more time—" His eyes turned ghoulish. "—but Miss Young said skip it. Being my employer's faithful boy, I skipped. Then Miss Young read tonight's paper."

An unpleasant chill developed in my gut region. "Read what?"

"About this riot. In Osterwald's toy department."

"What the hell's that got to do with me?"

"Listen, creep, don't play it so cute. The first time I went after Todd, I lost him in that same store. In the toy department, of all the screwy places. Miss Young thought Todd or somebody else was still carrying the papers. Then comes this news story tonight. About a party named Havoc, in Osterwald's. This Havoc steals some papers from the store—"

"Did the story say what kind of papers?"

He shook his head, showed me the crumpled ball from his pocket. "But there could only be one kind, shrimp, y'see?"

I saw, clearly and painfully. There was hardly any point in informing him that the papers described by the news sheet weren't the same ones he'd stashed in his pocket. I managed one more feeble squeak.

"Do you mean to tell me Ina Young wasn't worried about me until I went to Osterwald's today?"

"You look green, wart. That's just what I mean. Miss Young crossed you off completely. Sent me to hang around Todd's neighborhood. Some of the people there told me he was in a coma. I figured on waiting till he came out of it. Then I planned to beat the bejasus out of him. Even rough his wife up, if necessary, to get the stuff."

"You're nice. You truly are."

Merrily he told me what I could do with my sentiments and myself. He went on, "If I couldn't get the papers out of Todd, I was s'posed to learn the name of the guy who wrote the stuff. Miss Young was sure it wasn't your friend."

"It wasn't. He was just a patsy in the middle."

"So Miss Young figured. She wanted the papers first, then the author's name."

"So she could send you to kill him, thereby saving herself from Sharkey's mob?"

"My, you get smarter every sec, little man. Fat lot of good it'll do you. I'll just check the outdoors to make sure everything's nice and peaceful. Then I'll do what I came to do, and slip out the back way."

The sweat on my palms felt cold and sticky. Alfie marched to the blinds to the right of the door. Casually he pried two slats apart with his muzzle. He surveyed the scene outside, then ambled back.

"Awright, Havoc. Stand up. Lace your hands behind your back and—what's so amusing?"

"You. Miss Young ought to come in person. And bring a brain to go along with that muscle you call a head."

His arm whipped up. "I don't need to use a bullet, wart. I can club you silly just as easy."

"Sure! Go ahead. Then go back to Miss Young and show her the papers. You can both congratulate yourselves, sit down and drink a glass of blood until the cops come."

"Cops?" Defiantly he dragged the wadded sheets out. "Listen, man. We're clean. I got the stuff."

"Correction, Alfie. You have the original copy. *One* copy only."

It took a space of seconds for this to penetrate the cartilage he employed for thinking. Some of his confidence leaked away.

"Lousy bluffer! This is the stuff. All of it."

I had a further inspiration. "Oh? Pry that wad apart. Look at the hand-written note."

Alfie juggled his heater while he did so. Poor Nedrow opened his mouth in astonishment, to contradict my bluff. I slid my right toe over to his left one and unobtrusively leaned all my weight down hard enough to fracture his foot bones.

Nedrow blanched and shut his eyes. Alfie's lips moved as he read the scrap of a note. And read it again.

"I don't see what you're driving at, Havoc."

"Isn't there a reference to 'future copies,' lamebrain?"

"Call me names one more time—"

"Lamebrain fits! Do you think I'd be silly enough to write out one copy and not keep another stashed for insurance in case something like this happened?"

Ugly belief lit his eyes. "Okay. Where's the other?"

"The other *two*. Before I tell you, we make a deal."

"No lousy puking deals with a little two-bit—"

"Then you can shoot me, bud!" I yelled. "Go on! Plug me right now! Because Nedrow here doesn't know where the other copies are."

"Oh my God no, mister, I don't know, I didn't even know there *were* any oth—*armf*." He subsided into a mumble of agony as I mangled his arch a second time.

Despite the lethal tension of the moment, I was gaining confidence. I had Alfie bamboozled and running a fraction scared. I kept after him.

"Shoot, Alfie! Bang bang and it's all over. But if I were you, I'd take a plane for Brazil right away. I wouldn't return to Miss Young and report mission accomplished, unless you suddenly want to slide from her favor a few days or weeks hence, when the other copies come to light. As I guarantee they will."

Once more his pin brain assimilated these bald lies. "What's the deal?"

"We go get the papers. After which, you take Nedrow and me to the airport."

"So you can skip?"

"For good," I said piously. "I know when I'm in over my head."

I only prayed Alfie would think I was scared enough to make such a lunatic bargain. A bargain that gave him all the aces—chief among them the chance to blow us to bits as soon as I delivered the imaginary copies.

On the other hand, perhaps he wasn't as much of a numskull as he acted. Was he putting on an equally good show? Planning to ventilate me while professing to bargain?

Either way, I stood to end up dead. I'd worry about that when the time came. What I wanted now was a way to escape from Manny's Gastric Heaven and make it to my joint across the street.

108

Alfie digested his lower lip a while longer. Then, with a scowl, he said, "Okay, Havoc. I don't want to screw up for Miss Young. Where's the stuff?"

"Do we get passage to the airport when you get the papers?"

His face turned blank. "Sure, Havoc. A deal's a deal."

The sadistic glitter under his narrowed eyelids gave him away. I realized it would be tricky, leading him up to that flat, but it was the only way now. He thought he had me. And he was ninety-five percent correct.

"We have to walk across the street. To my place."

Alfie accepted the statement without a murmur. He snapped off the diner light switch, plunging the place into blackness, except for a couple of bulbs in the kitchen. This illumination served to outline the nasty planes of his face. I shuffled to the front door with some hesitancy.

What if the whole plan went kaflooie? I was banking all my chips on provoking trouble when Alfie came up against Polo Rogers' boy stationed inside my digs.

What if Polo's boy had pulled out?

"My nerves are collapsing," Nedrow complained as we headed outside. "I need sauce."

"I'll give you a lead highball if you don't shut up," Alfie advised him. He herded us down the snowy sidewalk.

The flakes were fatter now, whiter, whirling and dancing through the beams of the streetlamps. Nowhere on the street did I see a vehicle parked, except mine.

Aha! I thought joyfully. FitzHugh's boys are plenty cagey. They're waiting inside the vestibule of the building.

There was nobody inside the vestibule of the building when we got there except the three of us.

In the upstairs hall, I fumbled for the key, muttering apologies for my clumsiness in a loud voice. Alfie said:

"Pipe down! You wake up anybody, you're finished."

"I wouldn't do a rotten thing like that, Alfie," I quivered, inserting the key in the lock and giving several loud wiggles and turns the wrong way. At last the panel moved inward. Alfie shouldered me to one side.

"Where's the light switch?"

"To your right. The first turns on the living room lamps."

Oh, Polo's boy, I thought fervently, *be there*—

I tensed in the dark, ready to bowl backwards against Nedrow and knock us both down the stairs out of the line of the bullets the moment Alfie saw the gunsel—

Flick went the lights. Two dingy lamps at either end of the daybed cast wan gleams.

"Quiet as a tomb," said Alfie, walking inside. "Well? What are you guys waiting for?"

Time to think of another plan. "Come on, Moe," I said in a glum voice.

Alfie kicked the door shut. He surveyed the oft-repossessed furniture. Now the only way to keep him from ventilating us was to stall until FitzHugh's coppers arrived. After what I'd done to him tonight, Fitz couldn't fail to send some of his most trusted to roust me out and haul me to jail.

Could he?

I rubbed my hands together. "Anybody care for a little snort before we get down to business?"

"I'll snort you!" Alfie barked. "The papers!"

"Believe me," I said, "under the circumstances I'm fully as anxious as you to get all the copies off my hands. But why don't I call the airlines first and see about reservations for Nedrow and me? We'll leave town tonight—"

"The *papers!*" Alfie screamed with single-minded savagery.

In a tenth of a second I knew where it had to be hidden —the coat closet.

In that dark cubicle reposed my seldom-used golf clubs. I crossed my mental fingers and walked, hoping I'd have time to grab a driver, whirl and brain the gunsel before his superfast reflexes flexed.

It seemed to take the major part of fifty thousand years to reach that closet. Alfie breathed noisily. Nedrow held private conversations with himself on how unfortunate it all was. I grabbed the closet knob, turned it—

Nedrow let out a moan; I yelled something equally inane; and Alfie's blued cannon whipped up—

All at the precise instant in which, out of the closet, tottered a pale and trembling Gulf Bayles.

Fifteen

BEFORE I COULD REACT, Alfie snagged my shoulder, gave
me a jerk and *whoppo,* I caromed against the outer wall
next to the window.

The gunman let Gulf examine the cannon at close
range. Old miserable Gulf was panting and sighing and
generally looking ready to expire. His expensive clothing
was wilted, and so was his personality.

"I dunno what's goin' on here, Hammock, but I surely
don't want any part of it, y'hear?"

"Who's this?" Alfie asked. "Some faggo friend of
yours?"

"I resent that!" Gulf complained. "I was merely payin'
a call."

"In the closet?" Alfie sneered.

At last! A heaven-sent opportunity to divert Alfie's mur-
derous attention from myself. "His name's Gulf Bayles.
He wrote that blackmail material."

"He did?" Alfie blinked. "I thought you did. By God,
I'm gonna start shooting unless somebody levels—"

"Gulf," I cut in. "This is Ina Young's torpedo."

"Ina Young's—?" Gulf's eyeballs extruded themselves.
"Oh dear Gawd amighty. I thought the voice sounded
kinda familiar."

My clever stratagem backfired when Alfie hauled me
up by the suit front and bashed me across the molars
with the gunsight. My head snapped back and I lost my
temper, punching furiously at the air.

"You dirty sonofabitch, I'll clobber you—"

He put me down, all right. With another whack in the
chops.

I jarred off the floorboards near the window. The room
resembled an unfocused view through a reflex camera.
Alfie dragged me up, snapped his elbow to the fore and
clipped me brutally in the Adam's apple. I doubled over,
coughing, and he hacked the back of my neck.

111

About to sag once more, I was propped up by one of Alfie's ham hands. The other exhibited the rod under my nose. None of the other guests had presence of mind enough to jump him while his back was turned.

"Havoc, I'm sick and tired of the runaround. Did you write this stuff or did he?"

Gulf rushed forward. "I did. I'm the one, Mr. Gunman."

Alfie released me. I nearly plopped on my face. He swung around, tickling Gulf's navel region with the gun barrel.

"Then you'll get it in the belly first."

Nervous tics erupted all over the pale playwright's puss. "Please don't! I still have many beautiful messages to give the world. I'm a writer, y'understand. A sensitive writer of—"

"Shut up and take it like a man!"

"But I don't *want* it! Really n' truly 1 don't."

"Then why'd you mess around trying to blackmail Ina Young?"

"Doin' that was a terrible mistake! I never meant to get involved with criminals and killin'. Look here, mister. You just 'low me to get away and I'll forget all about it, honest I will. I'll pack myse'f on the first plane down to Mobile and spend the rest of my days writin' verse dramas. You'll never see me again."

His plea might have been laughable if it hadn't been so pathetic. Alfie was clearly up to his eyeballs in confusing circumstances, too. Bayles kept on bleating like a gored goat.

"Tell you what, mister. I'll even give you back all the papers if I can get 'em from this no-count crook I've been waitin' for."

Triumphantly Alfie yanked the crumpled murder story from his pocket. "I got the original already. All I need are the copies. That's why we came over here."

"Copies?" Gulf burbled. "What copies?"

"The copies of this, Goddam it!"

"There aren't any copies, mister. I ought to know. I wrote the cussed thing."

"Bigmouth!" I hissed. "Wideyap! I was trying—"

Alfie whirled and gave me another whack across the conko. "Trying to con me, huh, Havoc?"

112

My molars sprang open for a retort. I thought better of it. The more I steamed him, the smaller my chance for escaping a shootout whose end was me plastered on the carpet. I craned for a view out the window, mumbling:

"I give up, Alfie. I won't resist. Yes, I tried to con you."

"Are there any copies or not?"

"There aren't," I said. "But I didn't know Bayles was in here, Alfie. I swear I didn't."

From behind his tightly clutched Feend-O box, Moe Nedrow said, "Johnny, don't knuckle under to him."

"I don't see you doing the Light Brigade bit," I retorted.

"That's it," Alfie chuckled. "Tear each other apart. Makes my job easier."

"Ah, hell with it," I sighed, leaning my butt on the window sill. "What can I do, Nedrow?"

"About time you realized it," Alfie said.

I managed another squint down to the street. I noticed nothing but more snow a-dancing. Where in electric blue hell were the cops? Goodpasture was certainly slipping. Quickly I looked back to Alfie, asked:

"How about letting me ask Dixie boy a question or two?"

The gunman peeled back the cuff of his cashmere apparel, consulted his timepiece. "Go ahead. We might as well get this squared away so I can face Miss Young without looking like a jerk who doesn't have the answers." He redirected his muzzle. "But I'll ask the first one. Why the hell were you hiding in the closet?"

Gulf's gesture was theatrical. "I ducked in there 'cause I was scared. I heard you-all arrivin' and I got out of sight quick as I could."

"Hey!" I said, having a sudden flash. "Last night—were you here too? Bumbling around?"

The fragile and sensitive flower nodded. "I've been here ever since I ran into you in Wednesday's room at the hospital." For a trice defiance stiffened his scrawny shoulders. "Down home, we'd horsewhip a man from triflin' with another man's wife, y'know."

That settled one matter. Gulf, not Polo's henchman,

113

was the intruder. Alfie consulted his wristpiece again. "Don't gab all night."

Turning a soulful glance on our tormentor, Gulf whimpered, "Like I said, mister. I came here to find Havoc because I wanted those papers back. I figured he'd lifted them off his pal Basil Todd. If everythin' had gone right, I'd have beat him up, taken the papers and left town."

"And," Alfie emphasized, "there's only one set of papers?"

"Jes' one, right. So if you leave me go—"

Alfie laughed. "No dice. Now I can report back to Miss Young. Soon as I dispose of you, of course."

Practically popping my eyes out of their sockets, I strained for another glimpse of the street below. A car was approaching.

I sucked in a tense breath. Then I let it out. The taxicab cruised on.

A dead stillness gripped the apartment for a second. The reaper drew nearer with every loud tick of Alfie's watch. I tried to think of something to say. He beat me to the punch.

"Line up, all three of you. Over against that wall."

"Alfie, one more question!" I burst out. "I'd like to know how Bayles got involved in a blackmail plot. Obviously he doesn't have the belly for it. Don't you think Miss Young also would want to know?"

He thought that over while all of us listened to the silence in the building. Alfie turned. "Well, faggo?"

Gulf colored, clamped his lips together, walked over and sat down on the credit-financed sofa. He realized fury was futile. He shook his head, leaned his pale brow on the palm of his hand and talked to his shoelaces:

" 'Twasn't blackmail to begin with. It was literature. I was sleepin' off a big drunk at The Aphrodite, okay. And I was plenty scared when I ran out after you and the lady moved the body of that gangster. But I didn't plan on tellin' anybody. Y'see, I was worried about my career. My last three plays haven't done so well. These damnyankee critics got a personal vendetta goin'. So my agent persuaded me to try some other medium. After I recovered from the shock of bein' in the same room with a passion murder, I wrote a little short story."

114

"The blackmail mess?" Alfie inquired.

Gulf nodded. "It was the same story, but in the first version all the names 'n places were phony. Then I went to visit my wife in the hospital. For a loan. I had the manuscript in the pocket of my overcoat. I was goin' to show it to my agent. Well, I hung the coat on a rack in one room, went in to see my wife, and when I went to leave, after the bitch turned me down flat, I dug in my pocket and—and no story."

Despite the dull ache in my dome, another light was penetrating. "Bet I know who had it."

"That white trash Celebreese," Gulf said. "He was waitin' for me in the hall."

Thereupon Alfie demanded to know who the ringding hell Celebreese was. I filled him in briefly. Gulf went on with the rest of his lethally simple story.

Hunting for loot in a stranger's pocket, Dunc had come across the story script and recognized the physical description of the murdered man as tallying with the description of Liam Sharkey which had been plastered in the news rags for days. Foolishly, Gulf admitted now, he had kept the bit about Ina Young stabbing the man through the throat intact, even though the story people had fictitious names. That detail also helped Dunc fit the pieces together. Dunc suggested—in fact, as Bayles reported it, insisted upon—blackmail.

"I had to tell him everythin'!" Gulf protested. "Otherwise, he swore he'd get in touch with those hoodlums Sharkey hung 'round with, and they'd fix my wagon after they got me to tell what I knew. So I spilled my guts. I 'greed to rewrite the story usin' the right names. We'd send it over to Miss Young for money. Duncan had some ideas about tryin' to blackmail the mobsters too. I talked him out of it. I figured it'd be safer to tackle a woman."

Alfie's chuckle was brittle-hard. "You don't know Miss Young very good."

I broke in to tell Gulf that Dunc had been stiffing Polo's bunch on his own hook, and was, as a result, dead. Gulf's eyebrows shot skyward in dismay. Alfie allowed as how Dunc had received exactly what he deserved. Gulf said it only went to show what a mistake the whole caper was. The only person with no opinion was Moe

Nedrow. He stood in the corner holding the box, mummi-
fied.

And where were the cops?

"I would never have blackmailed the lady, mister,"
Gulf told Alfie. "B'lieve me, I wouldn't, 'cept I needed the
money. I'm a sensitive artist. I can't take any ordinary,
dirty job. I thought Miss Young'd be a soft touch. She's
a woman. An' she killed her man in the heat o' passion
and all. I thought she'd go right to pieces once she
cooled down."

"Not Miss Young," Alfie said, stroking his heater's
muzzle. "But you won't have to worry about a job any
more, sweetheart. If you gents are finished gassing—"

"Not quite," I said desperately. "There's the matter of
my friend Basil."

Unfortunately that part of the tale didn't take as long
as I'd anticipated. Gulf reported that dragging Basil in
had been Dunc's idea. Dunc suggested that he and Gulf
stay completely clear of Ina Young. Basil, a penniless
painter, would make a perfect messenger boy.

They conned Basil into believing that he was deliver-
ing some sort of paper requesting Ina's testimony at the
forthcoming Wednesday/Gulf divorce trial. But Basil told
Gulf and Dunc he couldn't visit The Aphrodite Club that
night. Or any night. He was playing Santa on a certain
corner, to make extra bucks and finance his way to art
school.

Bingo! That set off another flash in Dunc's twisty mind.
Basil should tell Ina that her answer to the fifty grand
demand must be delivered by eight that same night, to
unwitting Basil, on his corner. Only they didn't tell him
it was a fifty grand demand. They instructed him to use
the phrase, "a yes or no answer."

Trusting old Basil, familiar with Wednesday's prominence, figured it was all very legal and hush-hush and
asked no further questions. Dunc promised to cover for
Basil at the hospital in the afternoon if Basil would go
immediately to Ina Young.

I was getting slightly dizzy, both from tension and
Gulf's monotonous drawl. Now he was back to his original
theme.

"I know you feel you havta use that gun, mister. But

116

I swear before God, I was just tryin' to make an innocent dollar and get outa—"

"Will you quit *whining*?" Alfie slapped Gulf in the jaw. "I'm sick of that molasses drawl. Yawl this, yawl—what's *that*?"

I too heard the faint shuffle-scuffle in the hall.

Alfie stared at the door. I yelled, "The bulls, you crumb!" and dove past him.

I twisted the knob. Alfie turned purple. He raised his cannon, hand shaking. He wasn't sure if he should shoot it out with police.

"Officers," I babbled, running into the hall, "officers, by God I'm glad to see—oh *no*.

"Lothar, shove the little crud out of the way," said Polo Rogers.

Lothar clipped me in the side of the head. I went spinning. Polo shouldered out of the darkness, .45 at the ready.

"I took care of a couple of blue boys just pulling up downstairs and I—who the Christ are you?" he finished, confronting Alfie. Lothar crowded up close behind his chief, similarly armed. On the next floor above, a neighbor started complaining about the racket.

"I've seen you guys before," Alfie breathed, eyes wide. "In the papers or—"

"It's Polo Rogers, Sharkey's man," I bawled. "Polo, that man's boss killed Sharkey and—"

Ka-*bam*.

Alfie and Polo realized simultaneously that the other was the enemy. The blue cannons flashed.

Polo and Alfie both missed. I was halfway to Lothar's side, aiming to grab his gun, when Alfie went into a crouch and fired a second shot. Polo missed again but Lothar went down just as I reached him.

Fast and deadly, Alfie shot again. Polo made it three misses in a row as the explosions crashed one on another. Polo stumbled backwards, hit in the left shoulder, twisting around. He fell against me. Alfie leaped forward, smashed at Polo's gun wrist.

The .45 skated through the air, plopped on top of Lothar's chest. Sprawled out, Lothar didn't mind. Lothar was drilled between the eyesockets.

117

Polo's cheeks bleached out. He leaned against the door, his shot arm awkward as a doll's. So many things happened then, I had a hell of a time sorting them out.

The hallway lights flashed on. The guy and gal from upstairs, all pajamas and pincurlers, peeked over the rail and screamed something about World War III. Alfie fastened his free hand around my throat, his face a study in sadistic glee.

"Jump me, Havoc!" he whispered. "Jump me and I guarantee every one of your neighbors who butts in will get it before you."

That burned me so bad I could only splutter the worst curses I knew. But Alfie didn't mind the swear words. They amused him. While Polo groaned, he whipsered:

"I got ya, Havoc. Underneath all that showoff crap you're a yella coward. Now march. You too, Rogers!" He kicked Polo in the behind and the gangster tumbled down the steps to the landing below.

Propelling me forward, Alfie watched the stairs leading upward. No neighbors were in sight. Then Alfie remembered the other occupants of the room. He dragged me back. Nedrow hadn't changed position.

"Come on lardy," Alfie called. "Shake it up and— stand still, Bayles!"

Foolish Gulf made a dodge for the hallway that led into the efficiency kitchen. He kept running when Alfie ordered otherwise. Alfie calmly pumped out a shot that pierced Gulf's neck and sent him against the wall, sodden and dead.

Ramming me ahead of him down the stairs, Alfie shouted for all the apartment doors to hear: "Anybody sticks his Goddam head out gets it shot off!" Then, whispering, "Havoc, you help Rogers up."

There was no time nor room to protest, unless I wanted to get Nedrow murdered, plus a few of the people I heard whispering fearfully behind their doors as we marched down to the street level vestibule. Polo moaned, off his rocker with pain as he stumbled along beside me.

On the ground floor we cut through the building to the alley entrance, and Alfie's sedan.

Nedrow climbed mechanically into the back, still grasping the toy box. Polo tumbled in after him, cursing.

118

"Drive, Havoc." Alfie pushed me under the wheel.
What a mess! Polo half bled to death. Nedrow with the
weeping jimjams. But I got in, started the car.

Alfie brushed snow off his collar. He consulted his
watch one more time.

"What d' you know. Two in the morning already. Nice
time for a triple murder. Huh, Havoc?"

Sixteen

"TAKE CARE of yourselves, bums. I'll be back as soon as
I phone Miss Young and tell her about the catch I
bagged."

And with a wave of his rod and a sadistic smirk at our
collective expense, Alfie slammed the thick door. A bolt
rammed home on the other side.

Sunk on a red-upholstered chair and pale as a fish's
undergut, Polo clutched the gooey bright sleeve of his
coat. He gasped, "Check it, Havoc."

"What do you think I'm doing?" I twisted the brass
handle. "No dice. Locked solid."

"If only the bastard hadn't winged me," Polo breathed.
"What a Goddam indignity."

For the first time since Alfie had herded us up to the
fourth floor of The Aphrodite Club, Moe Nedrow showed
a sign of life. He peered over the top of the toy box and
said, "Is that all you can think about, indignity? How dignified are we gonna look at the funeral home? Havoc, this
is all your fault."

"Shut up, you robber. You asked for a cut of the pie.
Let me look around a second. There's bound to be
some way out."

Good old silly Havoc, whistling past the cemetery stones.
I didn't really believe what I'd just said. And neither did
they.

Nedrow plopped down in another chair under one of
the phony gaslights that gave the velvet walls of the private dining room a misty Victorian air. Polo ground his
teeth and cursed his luck in profane, pained syllables. I

hotfooted here and there, searching for another entrance.

There wasn't another entrance. Only the thick, black oak door Alfie had slammed and bolted.

Dispiritedly I yanked the pulls of the heavy black velvet draperies. Even before they swirled aside I knew what I'd see on the street, because I rememembered my first visit: iron bars.

The pavement below—four stories below—was dark and shiny wet. I had no trouble prying up the window, but that was as far as it went. Even I wasn't miniature enough to squeeze between the uprights. Behind me, Polo burbled:

"Chrissake, there must be *somebody* down there. Yell, Havoc. Scream. We *gotta* get out."

"Save it, big man. In the first place, this is a daytime district. Little shops. Second, it's now two thirty-five in the morning." I scrunched against the wall and peered up the dark thoroughfare from an angle. "All I see is one lone taxicab parked at the stand down on the corner. Way, way down on the corner."

"Try shouting," Nedrow suggested. "Try anything. I'm too wholesome to die."

"Aren't we all." I estimated the distance. "It's no use. The cab's windows are shut. Even if they weren't, four stories plus half of a long, long block is too far for a yell to carry."

I clapped the window shut in disgust. I extracted a crushed weed from my Brooks, lit up and tried not to notice that my own fingers were beginning to quake visibly. This, indeed, looked like the windup of the short, acquisitive career of J. Havoc, the pitcher who went to the well of money once too often.

"We can't just sit here and wait for the bastards to kill us!" Polo exclaimed. "You're such a smart operator, think of something!"

"That smartness, Polo, is sometimes merely a lot of yak to throw guys like you off balance. I'm blank."

An uneasy silence. I padded around the thick carpet, eyeing the few pieces of gingerbread furniture. This being the club's upper floor, we were apparently in a dining room that wasn't used often. Most of the chairs were covered with a film of dust. All the pieces looked old and,

120

worse, fragile. I probably wouldn't even dent Alfie's dome if I slugged him with one.

"Well," I said, "let's not lose hope. Something will happen."

That went over terrifically, as you might imagine. I puffed on the butt, approached Polo.

"Not that it'll do me much good, Rogers. But I'm curious about a couple of things."

Polo grimaced, gingerly fingered his bloody sleeve. "Curious! Jesus, what a time to be curious."

"How come you showed up at my joint tonight?"

"Simple," he wheezed, interspersing his answer with winces indicating his extreme pain. "I had your place staked out, from the roof, just to see you didn't play any cute tricks on me. My boy Lothar seen you go in that diner across the street. He called me. I wanted to settle up for what you did to Myron. The people in the subway gave him such a walloping, even the Blue Cross group policy I keep for the boys won't cover everything."

I nodded. "Okay. Next question. Why did you sell me out?"

Despite his gushing arm, Polo managed a look of juvenile innocence. "Sold whom out?"

"Listen, Rogers! This is no damn time to dance the minuet. You sold me out with an anonymous call to the police."

He raised his good hand placatingly, the fingertips unpleasantly gummed with red stuff. "Awright, lay off. That yellin' makes the arm hurt worse. I did tip the cops. But I planned to do it from the minute I let you out of my apartment."

"Nice guy. So bleed. Be my guest."

"Don't get huffy, Havoc. We're in this together. I had you pegged for a shifty hustler. Figured you'd doublecross me first chance you got. So I jumped first. I wanted the goods on Liam's killer. I thought that if I let you go, you wouldn't—or couldn't, with your rep—get me in Dutch with the cops. I let you go to set you up for a sellout. I knew I'd made the right move when you ditched Myron in the subway. I went ahead with my plan—"

"—by phoning the bully boys."

"Yeah. I tipped you into custody for one reason only. So I could spring you from jail."

I wagged my head. "I'm cracking up. You sold me out to *spring* me?"

Polo's knobby puss bobbed up and down. "Right. I was gonna help you get out of the country, see? Airplane to Mexico City, something like that. In return, you'd give me the name of the bum who called Liam."

In spite of the grim moment, I managed a feeble laugh. "Jokes on you, Polo. I didn't know the killer's identity. Then."

"I was ready for that, too. If you didn't know it by the time I was ready to spring you, I'd have just let you rot in the pokey."

"Pardon me for being obtuse, Polo, but that seems a hell of a roundabout way."

"Nuh-uh. Like I told you, little man. I knew your rep. And when you said you'd clam up if I started beating the truth out of you, I believed you. You got a funny kind of guts, Havoc, for a small guy."

"I'm so flattered I could weep buckets."

"Well, I mean it, Havoc. I figured that if I leaned on you, I might wind up with one more corpse on my hands, the way I did with Dunc Celebreese. But if you were in the clink—desperate—why, man, you'd be putty, just putty in my hands."

"All this is fascinating, Polo, except for one detail. Your gall. Your infernal gall in thinking you could bust me out."

His lips wrenched in a pastiche of a smile. "Hell, no problem. Liam Sharkey's organization is a big operation, boy. Coast to coast. Contacts and connections everywhere. Even in jails."

"I don't see the mob rushing to our aid right now."

Polo looked crestfallen. "We ain't used to dealing with dames."

There was little more he could offer in the way of enlightenment. I left him muttering about his need for medical attention. He was growing whiter every second.

I made another circuit of the room, pummeling my so-called brains for an answer to the problem of escape. As I marched past Nedrow, I noticed he was sitting even more stiffly than before, staring into space.

"Hey. Moe? You all right?" I touched his shoulder.

One fat tear trickled down his cheek. "I shoulda been a pawnbroker, Claudio."

"My God, don't start bawling."

"It's Finishville. For all of us."

I opened my trap to tell him otherwise, but unfortunately couldn't think of a reasonable argument to support the statement. Footsteps thudded softly in the hall.

Growing progressively more dazed, Polo rolled his eyeballs at the portal. Nedrow continued to hang on to the toy box like a tot afraid of losing his pacifier. He paid no attention as the bolt whacked back.

Ina Young marched in on red high heels.

"Well, well. The three bears."

The last time we'd met, she had looked tough but friendly. Now she merely looked tough, and a mite sleepy. Her cheeks were covered with hastily applied orange make-up. Her mouth was loaded with half a pound of raspberry lipstick. Snow crystals sparkled and melted in her copper-wire hair. There was a nasty little smirk at the corners of her mouth as she thrust her hands into the pockets of her mink jacket and surveyed us. Alfie darted in after her, cannon ready.

"Havoc, you weren't very smart, mixing in this," she said.

"Tell me something else fascinating, lady."

"He thinks he's cute," Ina said over her shoulder.

"He'll find out," Alfie replied ghoulishly.

"You're the one," Polo wheezed. "You're the one who gave it to Liam."

"That's right!" she spat. "We had a great thing going for almost three years. Then the two-timing sonofabitch tried to tell me we were finished. Oh, he'd fooled around before. Men are that way. But he always came back to Ina. Until this time. This time, he came back to say he was bugging out on me permanently. He tried to tell me he'd found what he really wanted in a woman in some dolly named Vanessa. Nobody tells Ina Young that," she finished coldly.

"If I wasn't bleeding to death," Polo gasped, "I'd walk over there and wring your jealous neck."

Ina laughed. "Save your strength. I want you to be

123

alive to enjoy the sensation of heading into a nice grave in the river. You and your two pals."

"What are you, for Christ's sake, a woman or a machine?" I yelled. "There are two dead bodies already tonight. Going to make it three more?"

Ina laughed again. "Little man, I'm out to chalk up a record to match St. Valentine's Day."

"She's not kidding," Nedrow breathed. "She *means* it."

I kept quiet, but he was painfully right. There was an all-steel glint in Ina Young's eyes that was pure homicide. She'd gored Sharkey with a fork, and she was determined there'd be nobody left alive who knew her secret. She hooked a thumb at the paralyzed Nedrow.

"That fat slob I've never seen before. Who is he, Alfie?"

"Some friend of Havoc's. In cahoots with him, trying to get the papers."

Ina strolled over to me. "Oh, yes. The papers. Well, little man, Alfie turned those over to me the minute I arrived. Right now there's nothing left of them except some gray ashes in the fireplace down in the cocktail lounge. Tell you the truth, the first time you came to see me, I had you figured as legitimate."

"I more or less was," I said. "Look, as long as this is the end of the line, fill me in. Call it morbid curiosity. What happened when Basil brought you the goods and the note demanding the fifty thou?"

The shoulder of Ina's mink jacket lifted in a shrug. "I opened the envelope and got the surprise of my life. When I got mad and showed your friend the material, he looked as surprised as I was. But he wouldn't tell me who sent him. I called Alfie. We tried to muscle him a little. He grabbed the envelope and ran out of the office."

"I'd have fried him on the spot," Alfie put in, "except for the damn decorators."

"So you chased him," I said. "And lost him in Osterwald's."

And, I finished mentally, Basil ditched the envelope in the nearest convenient place—a Feend-O box just arriving on a cart—after he lost Alfie and calmed down enough to decide he didn't want goods like that on his person.

"Before he ran out, did Basil say he wanted an answer by that night?"

"Correct," Ina snapped. "He told us where to deliver the answer, too. The exact streetcorner."

Alfie scowled. "Only I found you instead, hustler."

Now, finally, it all made sense: Basil told Ina, per orders from Dunc and Gulf, that Ina must deliver "her answer" by eight o'clock. But he was scared. He ran to the Unicorn's Den, got drunk, doodled the napkin and fell downstairs on his way home. Olive jingled me. I took the corner and—

Of such circumstances are funerals made.

I noticed Ina watching me with a peculiar curiosity. "Like I said, Havoc. When I turned the screws on Todd, he blurted out that he was a mural painter, not a crook. Then you showed. I was convinced you didn't know a thing about the blackmail plot. So I invented a story on the spot about the paint-pot boy wanting a job. After all, we *were* redecorating."

She smiled, grotesquely amused. "The whole job's a cover for tearing up the dining room downstairs where that lowlife Sharkey got his. He spattered blood all over. I had to redo the place, actually hire a whole crew of painters and plasterers, to make the cover story stick— I told 'em I'd tried out all sorts of paint samples in that one dining room. I did, too. Slapped it on right over the blood."

I shook my head. "That's a lot of trouble."

Again the cold shrug. "I didn't want a coast to coast organization after me."

With a sad look at Polo folded into his chair and breathing hard, I told her, "Don't mind my saying so, but it strikes me you're tougher than half dozen Polos wrapped in one. When you want to be."

Ina dipped her copper curls. "Thanks for the compliment. Are you referring to right now, for instance?"

"You're not seriously contemplating three more dead bodies—"

"I'm not contemplating anything else." She backed off a step. "Keep that gun on him, Alfie. He's got the nervous rabbit look."

No wonder. For the first time, I saw how miserably heartless the broad was.

Alfie scratched his nose. "The river means a truck to haul them away. No dirtying the cars."

"Can you get a truck?"

"I got a friend who works in a brewery across town. Take me about half an hour."

Ina nodded. "I'll wait down in the office. They can't get out of here anyway. Set yourselves right with the world, gentlemen. Thirty minutes and it's all over."

Turning, she marched out into the hall. Alfie followed, and bolted the door.

"Do something," Moe Nedrow wailed. "Do *anything*. Put me out of my misery."

"Tell me what to do!" I yelled hotly. "That door's practically steel. There's no other entrance, unless one of you jerks can fly out through those bars. Personally, I never learned the Peter Pan bit."

Polo uttered a flatulent gasp and rolled his eyes up in the sockets, close to passing out. Nedrow began a long monologue, weepingly delivered, about the more sensible life of a pawnbroker. Approximately thirty minutes to save our triple hash and what troops did I have to do it with? One stretcher case and one basket case.

And me with absolutely no ideas.

Down below I heard a car pull away.

Alfie, after the truck.

I walked over to the wall, doubled up my fist in anger and began pounding the maroon velvet.

Bang, bang, *bang*.

I pounded the wall until my knuckles ached like hell. I'll admit it wasn't a very practical gesture.

But it was the best I could manage in the light of a situation that was totally hopeless.

Seventeen

ONCE MORE I wandered to the window. I grappled with the bars in a vain attempt to wrench them bodily from their cement sockets. All I got for my trouble was abused palms.

I squinched against the wall, peered along the street again. The lone Yellow was still at the stand, dome light gleaming. I saw the dim shape of the cabbie inside.

There was help. *There* was a way out.

But yelling would only bring Ina running to silence us. All sorts of lunatic notions flashed through my conk.

Telepathy?

Flying paper airplanes down four stories?

Nothing would help. The cab stand looked further and further away every time I looked at it.

Gnashing my mental teeth, I swung around and said to nobody in particular, "Dammit, if we only had some way of reaching that guy parked on the corner, we could—"

Then complete idiocy struck.

But *was* it idiocy?

I stumbled forward, fingers wiggling out ahead, reaching.

Nedrow recoiled in his chair. "You've gone crazy, Havoc. Halp! Mister Gangster, he's gonna strangle me—"

"I never believed it," I whispered. "I never believed I'd ever be glad I watched a commercial. Nedrow, let me have that—"

And I wrested the toy container from his clutching fingers.

Sweating to beat hell, I turned the box round and round until I found the copy line and ran my finger along it.

"See, Nedrow? Feend-O the Ferocious, with wireless remote control *up to one eighth of a mile.* By God, it better be true, because we're going to try it."

"Oh, you've really gone flippola, Havoc."

"Be quiet! Got a pen on you?"

Polo watched dumfounded while I ripped at the lid of the carton and extracted the plastic monster. Indicating me, Polo agreed with Nedrow: "Bound to happen. He's gona gaga."

"All right," I snarled, fanning back Nedrow's lapel and dragging out a ballpoint I discovered there. "You two can call me crazy. This is our only chance—"

I knelt on the floor. I laid Feend-O prone and tried to ignore the malevolent stare of his mechanical eyes as I tested the ballpoint on the flat plastic expanse of his chest. The point made an inky blue squiggle. I printed, fast as I could, in block letters:

HELP! SEND POLICE TO APHRODITE CLUB. LIFE AND DEATH. THIS IS NO GAG.

Then I set Feend-O up on his roller feet and ran to the window.

"Come on, Nedrow! Help me!" I hauled at the draperies, yanking them bodily off the hooks. "I need a long rope to lower that plastic dummy to the sidewalk. Tear up the drapes! Make yourself useful!"

A spark of hope gleamed in Nedrow's blue eyes. He rushed to assist. My insane activity must have pushed Polo into the pit of despair, for he buried his eyeballs in his palms and began to sob plaintively.

The drapes were tough to tear, but after about five frantic minutes, we'd rent apart enough long strips to make a decent rope. We knotted the segments together. I formed a loop with which I proceeded to string up Feend-O by his plastic neck.

Crossing mental fingers, I shoved the creature at the bars.

"He fits!" I crowed as Feend-O sailed into space. "Hang onto that rope, Nedrow."

Moe blinked. "Rope? Aren't you holding the rope?"

"Oh Christamighty!" I sprawled full length on the carpet, grabbing the tag end of the velvet chain a second before it sailed through the bars.

I hit my dome on the window sill but held on. I clambered to my feet, tugged tentatively on the line. I felt a weight on the end of it, but it was impossible to see Feend-O because of the angle of the front of the building.

"Thank God he didn't smash on the sidewalk. Hold on, now. Gently, gently—"

And I paid out the rope until the weight at the end went ka-*bump*.

"He's down. I hope to God he's upright."

Frantically I rushed across the room, latched onto a chair and the small multi-knobbed plastic control unit. I jammed the chair against the sill and climbed up. From that angle I could still see only half of the sidewalk. That half didn't contain Feend-O.

"If I dropped him down a window well we're sunk," I said, flipping the *On* button.

Drifting up from below came a faint mechanical whine, *garowwwwwWWWW*, as Feend-O's innards warmed up. A weak yellow light flickered across the strip of wet sidewalk. I twisted the *Walk* control.

128

Into my field of vision marched that beautiful creature, bulbous eyes rotating and glowing, grasping arms swinging backward and forward, velvet rope dragging behind him.

In my haste I spun the *Walk* knob too far. Wheels turning like mad, Feend-O hurled toward the curb.

"Stop, back up, reverse!" I cried wildly, fingering the dial.

Feend-O tottered on the edge of the curbing, was momentarily in danger of falling prone on his puss on a sewer grating.

I cut the power just in time.

He began to back up at an alarming speed.

I discovered that the way you held the control unit determined the way the little plastic monster walked, but I had him going half a block in the wrong direction before this fact became apparent.

"Is he turned around?" Nedrow whispered, cheeks jammed against the bars.

"Almost, almost. Wait—there he goes. Okay, Feend-O. Go, buddy. Go save our bacon."

Properly oriented, the bug-eyed thing began to trundle toward the distant taxi stand. I managed a feeble smile.

"It's working, Moe! He'll make it if the power holds out—"

The taxi stand with its lone vehicle appeared to be more distant than the other side of the moon, however. Feend-O's progress, even at top speed, was alarmingly slow. Back, forward went his arms. Little spears of yellow light shot out of his revolving eyeballs. An eighth of a mile? It looked more like eight miles.

"Twenty minutes gone already," Nedrow whispered. "That blond brute'll be back any time."

"Be quiet!" I had my map plastered against the bars. "Feend-O'll make it. Feend-O's my baby. Feend-O's going to come through for all of us."

"I don't want to get my hopes up," Nedrow complained. "That way, I'll feel all the worse when those two murderers walk in here and murder—what's wrong?"

"There's a guy on the pavement. He just staggered out of a doorway. Oh, God. A *drunk*."

Practically in tears, I watched the old coot capering a couple of yards ahead of Feend-O. He craned his head forward to peer at the frightening contraption rolling hell-bent for him.

The drunk wagged a finger, as if he were holding a private conversation with one of his booze visions.

Feend-O kept advancing, rotating his eyes, reaching out with his plastic claws.

All at once the drunk got scared. He aimed a kick at Feend-O's head. If he smacked him over, we were finished—

Desperately I twisted the control box around. Feend-O did an abrupt right face toward the gutter.

The drunk goggled, convinced he was face to face with the supernatural. He leaped over Feend-O's head, cried *"Yiiii!"* to the snowy darkness and went pelting past The Aphrodite to take the cure.

I wrenched the box around before Feend-O nosedived into the gutter. He was on his way again.

"Close call," I said. "Many more and I'll have a coronary."

A big, ugly tomcat strolled out of another sewer grating just as Feend-O got two thirds of the way to the corner.

Hastily I reversed the controls. Feend-O backtracked.

Pussy advanced, sniffing.

His right paw snaked out to give Feend-O a scratch in the map.

Feend-O tottered on his rollers, off balance.

Pussy jumped again. I meant to put the plastic job into full reverse. Instead, my fingers bollixed the job and Feend-O rushed forward full tilt.

His windmilling claws whacked pussycat right across the schnozz.

With a *fitz-rowrr* audible all the way up to where we were, the feline bounded off in the dark.

Upright still, Feend-O plowed on.

I closed my eyes and gulped. "He made it."

"Futile," Nedrow mumbled beside me. "The cab just pulled out."

"He *made* it! By God, good old Feend-O made it, he—*what did you say?*"

"The taxi," Nedrow repeated. "Somebody called the taxi. There it goes now."

I opened my eyes. I nearly broke down and bawled.

Sure enough, the cabbie had revved up and was even now U-turning on hissing tires. He belted out of sight down the cross street at the intersection. And there was little Feend-O, still manfully marching on to an empty corner.

There was no justice. Nedrow began to blubber. I drew the radio control unit back, preparatory to pitching it out through the bars in disgust. I spotted headlights far down the street, coming fast. Big headlights.

I didn't even have the strength the throw the control box away. "That truck," I wheezed. "It's Alfie."

Nedrow paid no attention. He'd shambled back to his chair, shaking his head. I watched with a kind of ghoulish fascination as the headlights speared wet paths along the pavement, two blocks away and racing.

Another moment, Alfie'd be at the intersection. Would see Feend-O trundling along rolling its damned electric eyeballs, in plain sight—

Somehow I couldn't tear my gaze from that hideous scene.

The lines of the truck had grown discernible now. It was a big panel job, one block away from the intersection.

I thought dully about trying to drive Feend-O into the gutter. What was the damned use? Alfie would be sure to spot the glow from its eyes, or the velvet rope dragging behind it, straight to the front of The Aphrodite Club.

The truck was half a block from the intersection.

A quarter of a block—

I shut my eyes and leaned against the bars, giving up.

I heard a double squeal of brakes, a growling of gears. I looked out.

My heart practically jumped out between my guns.

Alfie had swung his truck wide into the other lane, rammed on the brakes, to avoid hitting a taxi. A sweet and lovely new taxi that had popped around the corner and taken its place at the stand vacated by the preceding Yellow.

Alfie was too busy avoiding a near-crash to spot Feend-O, who now bumbled along approximately parallel with the taxi's front fender. Alfie gunned the truck past the Aphrodite Club and turned right, out of sight.

If only the cab had masked Alfie's view of the mechani-

131

cal contraption! And if only the cabbie would spot Feend-O now!

"Look around, dimwit!" I shouted. "Don't you see Feend-O right outside your cab?"

Who looks for walking toys on a public thoroughfare at past three in the morning?

Polo had lifted his head. He groaned feverishly. Nedrow stood against the wall, eyes popping.

"Havoc?" Nedrow breathed. "Havoc, here they come. In the hall—"

The taxi door remained closed.

Feend-O kept marching, abreast of the gas cap now. We were done. The raucous knocking on the bolted door merely emphasized it.

"You clowns stand back," Alfie sang out. "We're coming inside."

Dismally I faced around from the window. No point in watching Feend-O march into oblivion.

Polo tried to stand, but he was too weak. The portal swung back. In waltzed Ina, a cat-swallowing-cream grin on her lips. Alfie darted after her.

I moved midway across the room. Alfie shook his head and motioned me back.

"The transportation has arrived," Ina informed us blandly. "Go ahead, Alfie."

He sniggered, lifted his muzzle. "I can't decide which one to plug first."

Hallucination, I thought.

I'm hearing gears.

I'm hearing engines.

I'm hearing brakes.

I'm hearing soles on concrete.

I'm hearing a gravely voice yelling, "Hey, open up in there!"

Ina Young's eyes flared wide. "Who pulled the drapes down?"

"I said open up," came the gravely voice. "This is cab driver Ginkowitz. What's going on?"

Ina Young turned white. "Jesus Christ! The downstairs door—"

A ferocious knocking began. The cries of cabbie Ginkowitz were masked by Ina's low, dirty cursing. She ran to the window.

"There's a rotten cab out in front!"

Somehow the cabbie had seen Feend-O! Somehow—

Alfie's face was working hatefully, even as he swung the rod to cover all three of us at once, an impossible task. Suddenly Ina cried, "These idiots must have hung the drapes out—"

"Ginkowitz!" I shouted, drowning her out the second I jumped her.

I crooked one arm around her neck, dragging her back against the open window. Over my shoulder I hollered, "Call the cops on the cab radio, Ginkowitz!"

Alfie was so unnerved he flipped up his heater and his trigger finger went white.

"Don't shoot *me,* Goddam it!" Ina bawled.

She kicked my shins like a madwoman. I gave her a shove that hurtled her forward. She staggered on her high heels, cursing, struck Alfie broadside. His cannon went off.

I hit the carpet. The slug blasted a hole out of the wall above my head. Alfie tumbled over, off balance. Ina Young scrambled up, unclasping the handbag over her arm. Presto, there was a small, wicked lady's pistol in her paw.

Her face writhed as she spun to meet the new assault —Polo had managed to struggle to his feet, was running at her, face contorted, hands outstretched for her throat.

Ina drilled him between the eyes.

I did a flying tackle and clobbered Alfie amidships, hurling him against the wall again. His killing instinct was working overtime. He batted at me with his big fist, and would have taken my head off except that I ducked out of the way. The force of his punch made him spill over prone. I stamped my insole down on his wrist.

Alfie dropped his cannon. I snatched it up, catching a flicker of movement in the corner of my eye. I dropped on one knee, twisted and fired, the second Ina Young's little nickeled pistol went off.

My slug caught her in the left hip, lifted her off the carpet, sprawled her on her back. Her bullet sent one of the imitation gaslights into tinkling ruin.

I climbed to my feet, shaking my head.

In the distance I heard the beautiful scream of a siren.

"Good old Ginkowitz," I muttered, close to passing out with shock. "Good old police and good old—Nedrow, what's wrong with you? Why are you staring at me like—

Staring and flapping his arms, and suddenly I read the dangerous message he was trying to scream but couldn't.

Over Ina's moans I heard a clink of glass, an obscene oath. I stumbled out of Alfie's path just as he leaped at me with a fragment of the lamp glass held like a knife.

The edge sliced my cheek, fiery as hell. I jigged unsteadily, tumbling over my own feet, and suddenly I remembered how he'd first worked me over, pushed me around because I was undersized. That's why, just as he pulled up short of where I'd fallen, and turned for another attack, I pumped three shots up into his jaw.

Alfie pitched over on top of Polo Rogers. They couldn't have made a nicer pair of deads.

The siren howled closer.

More brakes complained.

Vaguely I heard cabbie Ginkowitz exchanging loud remarks with the minions who trampled across the sidewalk and began to smash in the door four stories down.

Nedrow was a sight, chewing his nails and blinking at me through the cordite smoke. All at once I noticed Ina Young trying to crawl toward the door. The wound in her hip was too bad. She fell back, gasping. Her tough eyes found me. They were still hateful. But they were defeated.

I dropped the rod on the carpet. Lying there caught, Ina Young called me two or three choice dirty names.

I thumbed my nose at her and passed out.

134

Eighteen

LET ME CITE to you, cousins, the injustice of it all.

What do I get, as a public-spirited citizen responsible for bringing Ina Young to justice?

First, a crummy patch-up job by a police doc. He plastered a bandage on my cheek after I came around in the midst of the carnage at The Aphrodite.

Next, a journey to a cell in the City Jail.

Then, an interview with FitzHugh Goodpasture.

I sat listlessly on my home-away-from-home metal cot. FitzHugh, professionally attired for grilling in rolled-up sleeves and moist Havana, paced up and down.

"This is it, Havoc. Yes sir, this is it. Do you want to confess?"

"Confess what? I got Sharkey's killer, didn't I? You said Ina Young did the confessing."

"That's right, but—"

"And I gave you Dunc Celebreese's killer too, didn't I? Even though he was chilled. You pick up Polo's playmate, Myron. He'll tell you about the kid."

"Oh, yes, we already have him," said FitzHugh, the picture of smugness. "We also have you."

"On what charge? Dammit, seems to me you ought to be treating me like a hero."

One by one he gloatingly ticked off his fingers. "Withholding evidence. Disturbing the peace. Inciting to riot."

I sighed and waved. "Ah, FitzHugh, you're just jealous."

"Am I? Let's begin with that little matter of practically causing a national emergency in the subway. Oh, yes, I have a full report on it. Havoc, I accuse you—"

He never got around to doing any accusing. There was a commotion outside the cell. A stentorian voice exclaimed, "Who's in charge, here?"

FitzHugh peered outside suspiciously. A portly gent in expensive duds waltzed into view behind the jailer.

135

"This is a disgrace! Coming down here and finding this fine young man locked up."

Could he mean *me*?

FitzHugh accosted the jailer, who was fitting a key in the lock. "Hold on there, Pomfret. I'm in charge here, Mr. Big-mouth. The name's Goodpasture. Detective Goodpasture. Are you a lawyer?"

"No, sir," said Portly with considerable acid. "I am Lemuel G. Soaper, publisher of the *Evening Trumpet*. Which, in case you don't know, is the newspaper which offered a ten thousand dollar reward for the apprehension of Liam Sharkey's killer."

Goodpasture goggled. "Sir—I—uh—this man is a sneaky, conniving—"

"Public servant!" Soaper interrupted testily. He reached through the bars. "Mr. Havoc, come here. Allow me to shake your hand. Also, I wish to pass into it this certified check for ten thousand dollars."

The publisher flung Goodpasture another glare. I darted to the bars and put on a winsome smile while exchanging shakes. A photographer popped into view. Soaper turned profile as the flashbulb exploded.

"It's certainly a shame," said the publisher, "when a public servant like this young man is held in jail and subjected to brutal police methods."

I pointed to my bandaged cheek. "Yes, sir. Look at this. They've been giving me the third degree."

"For God's sake!" Goodpasture exclaimed. "He didn't get that bandage here."

"Believe me," said Soaper, "I intend to expose this kind of municipal corruption in the *Trumpet*."

"Corruption?" Goodpasture turned purple. "Sir, you haven't any idea how this little wretch has twisted the law. Insulted it! Dodged it and—oh, no. No, no, *no!*" Goodpasture pounded the bars, realizing the game. "Not *this* time, Havoc. Bad press or no bad press, you're finished."

Soaper spoke up with authority. "Very well. Mr. Havoc, I'll have a battery of attorneys from the *Trumpet's* legal staff at your disposal within the hour. And will we have headlines!"

Another fearsome glare at the dismayed detective and Soaper tipped his hat. "Now, I think I'd best step aside to make way for the other visitors waiting."

"Other visitors?" Goodpasture echoed. "Pomfret, dammit, why—"

"Can't help it," said the jailer. "He seems to have lots of friends."

"Johnny old buddy, how are you, Claudio?" boomed a voice.

There was Nedrow leaning against the bars, fully restored to larcenous normality. He lamped the pink check I still held, grinned.

"Deal's a deal, remember. Half that's mine."

"Okay, okay," I said. "I'm no welsher. At least I'll make five grand on—"

The rest of the remark went unremarked. Among the other guests come to pay their respects, I spied a brimming-eyed Olive Todd. And, upright at last, big Basil, hickory shirt, broad grin, gauze-wrapped head and all.

"Johnny!" he said, close to bawling. "I heard what you did for me while I was laid out. I'm touched. I really am."

I began to suspect I was the party being touched. "Uh, how's that again, Basil?"

"Promising Olive here half of anything you recovered. The way I see it, that cash from the newspaper will just about cover my doctor bills, the art school tuition, and some toys for Murphy for Christmas. Poor little tyke, I thought he wouldn't have a happy holiday." Basil's face fell. "I've already bought the toys. Of course, if you weren't serious when you told Olive—"

What choice had I? "Sure I was serious, Basil."

Olive pressed my fingers through the bars. "Johnny, it's wonderful of you."

"Oh, think nothing of it," I said.

Me and my big yap! I'd talked away all ten thousand clams. But I couldn't back down, much as a greedy little devil inside me insisted I should. I'd certainly been through a hell of a lot to emerge totally profitless. But such, I consoled myself, are the vicissitudes of hustling.

Basil fixed Goodpasture with an unfriendly eye. "Detective, I happened to overhear what you said to Mr. Soaper a moment ago. Personally, I agree with him. This is a hell of a thing to do to my friend. Especially since he's shown himself to be a true patron of the fine arts."

"And especially since this is Christmas Eve," added Olive.

I blinked. "Already? I haven't even made out my shopping list."

Goodpasture snapped, "You think I *like* staying here? I'm supposed to be off duty today. My brother's coming in from Philadelphia. My wife's making eggnog and plum pudding. But I'm doing my job, staying here, trying to bring this mercenary crook to some semblance of justice."

"Scroogeville, Claudio," said Nedrow. "The bit fits, though. You look kinda finky to me."

"Pomfret! Clear all these people out of here so I can proceed with my interrogation of—now who the hell's *that*? This place is becoming a Goddam railroad station."

A feminine voice said, "But I tell you, officer, I'm his sister!"

A couple of drunks in the tank across the aisle whistled. "Wa*hoo*, baby. C'mon in and give old Sydney a li'l Christmas present."

"Vanessa!" cried I.

She thrust her toothsome self into the crowd, grinned and hoisted a cardboard parcel.

"I brought you a fruitcake."

"I'll take that, Miss." Pomfret reached. "Prisoners aren't allowed to have—"

"No!" Vanessa grabbed it away from him. The string popped. The fruitcake arched out of the box as the lid fell off. It struck the floor and split open.

I covered my eyes. Vanessa looked glum.

"I see," whispered Goodpasture, pointing at the spilled contents of the crumbly cake. "A file. A pistol. A box of bullets."

I peeked out from behind my hand. Honest to Arthur, there was all the stuff, wedged in between the nutmeats and the maraschino cherries.

"Polo told me I was supposed to help you escape!" Vanessa wailed.

Oh, mother. "Vanessa, that was *before* Polo got creamed. Don't you read the papers?"

"No. I was too busy buying the fruitcake and all the other stuff." She twiddled her gloves. "I'm sorry it was a bad idea."

A fiendish laugh escaped FitzHugh's lips. "Why, no, young lady. It was a dandy idea, just dandy. I'll have to find out all about it, right after I book Havoc on attempted escape." He swiveled his spaniel eyes to me. "This time—at last—"

"FitzHugh, be serious! Think I'd be dumb enough to plan a low comedy bit like that?"

"I don't *care*. Do you hear me? I don't care any longer, John Havoc. I've lost all my scruples, all my ideals, everything except my overwhelming, burning, intense and practically maniacal desire to see you in jail, jail, jail. *Forever!*"

Well, that was about the end. I was sunk.

"Johnnybaby?" someone trilled. "Where *is* the little doll?"

Then came a babble of voices, more protesting cries of officers on duty somewhere beyond the cell. All at once the hall was overflowing with sycophants, juvenile autograph seekers, reporters brandishing pads and—short and deliciously packed into a tight black dress—Wednesday Wilde.

"The paper said you were in jail, darling," she purred, offering me her juicy lips through the bars. Vanessa flounced out. I bussed Wednesday fondly and said it was true. She switched her hips, flung up one glove dramatically and announced, "Then that's where I want to be, too."

The crowd cheered. Flashbulbs went off. FitzHugh Goodpasture began to tremble.

"Make yourselves at home, folks," I said. "The more the etcetera."

Wednesday clapped her hands. "Johnny, I had the most wonderful idea. I've never cooked a meal in my life. But if you're cooped up in this horrid penal institution,

139

I'm going to make certain you have a yummy Christmas dinner."

She gestured down the aisle, where gape-jawed cons hung out the bars in amazement. "And all those nice gentlemen, too."

"Everybody get out!" FitzHugh screeched. "This is against the law—"

Wednesday ignored him. "All right, darlings. Bring in the portable ovens. Put the baskets of turkey down right there. Careful of those bottles of eggnog!"

"Three cheers for the broad!" cried one of the men in the drunk tank. "Huzzah, huzzah, huzzah!"

A reporter pressed through to the bars. "Mr. Havoc, I'm from *National Peephole*. As Miss Wilde's latest—ah—friend, naturally the editors are interested in your life story."

"They are?" Avarice awoke. "Well, I don't come cheap."

"A thousand dollars for six installments?" he suggested.

Another reporter shouldered him aside. "Don't sell! Two thousand from *Intimate Cinema*."

"Bid it up, boys," I said.

Suddenly there was a palsied hand on my shoulder. "Havoc?" Goodpasture quivered. "Havoc, I—I can't take it. I simply *cannot take it*. You're released. Merry Christmas!"

"Oh, I dunno about that, Fitz. I think the cons might like a nice holiday dinner. Is there any law against my staying here for a while?"

"Is there any law against—*Pomfret!* Let me out! *Quick!*"

He tussled his way through the mob scene. I cried Merry Christmas, but he was gibbering too loudly to hear.

Wednesday appeared at the bars and silently framed a few words with her appealing lips: "Christmas present. *Later.*"

"My hormonal pleasure," I said with a grin as she fitted her neat hips into an apron.

It got pretty crowded in that jail block, I'll say. What with portable ovens and eggnog, and Olive and Nedrow and Basil Todd getting palsywalsy, and Wednesday cooking, and the cons singing "Jingle Bells," and finally the

140

amazed, overwhelmed cops too, and me finagling the reporters into higher, ever higher prices for my syndicated autobiography—

Believe it or not, if I ever spent a merrier Christmas, I can't remember when.

THE END

Also available from
The Armchair Detective Library

Death in the Fifth Position by Edgar Box
Spider Kiss by Harlan Ellison
The Shakeout by Ken Follett
The Bear Raid by Ken Follett
Dead Cert by Dick Francis
Nerve by Dick Francis
For Kicks by Dick Francis
Licence to Kill by John Gardner
The November Man by Bill Granger
The Blessing Way by Tony Hillerman
The Fly on the Wall by Tony Hillerman
Dance Hall of the Dead by Tony Hillerman
Johnny Havoc by John Jakes
Havoc for Sale by John Jakes
The Big Bounce by Elmore Leonard
Hombre by Elmore Leonard
Rosemary's Baby by Ira Levin
The Scarlatti Inheritance by Robert Ludlum
Cop Hater by Ed McBain
The Mugger by Ed McBain
The Pusher by Ed McBain
First Blood by David Morrell
Crocodile on the Sandbank by Elizabeth Peters
The Curse of the Pharaohs by Elizabeth Peters
A Prospect of Vengeance by Anthony Price

Collector Edition $25 Limited Edition $75
(100 copies, signed, and slipcased)
Postage & handling $3/book, 50¢ each additional
A trade edition with library binding is also available.
Please contact us for price and ordering information.

The Armchair Detective Library was created in affiliation with *The Armchair Detective* and The Mysterious Press with the aim of making available classic mystery and suspense fiction by the most respected authors in the field. Difficult to obtain in hardcover in the United States and often the first hardcover edition, the books in The Armchair Detective Library have been selected for their enduring significance.

For the production of these editions, materials of the highest quality are used to provide a select audience with books that will prove as timeless as the stories themselves. The paper is 60–lb. acid free Glatfelter for longevity. The collector and limited editions are bound in heavy duty Red Label Davey Boards, encased in Holliston Roxite "C" grade cloth and Smyth sewn for durability.

Printed and bound by Braun–Brumfield, Inc. of Ann Arbor, Michigan, U.S.A.